Jim Crace is the author of *Continent*, *The Gift of Stones*, *Arcadia*, *Signals of Distress*, winner of the 1995 Royal Society of Literature's Winifred Holtby Memorial Prize, *Quarantine*, which won the 1997 Whitbread Award, and *Being Dead*. He has also received the Whitbread First Novel Prize, the E. M. Forster Award, the Guardian Fiction Award and the GAP International Prize for Literature. His novels have been translated into fourteen languages.

Jim Crace lives in Birmingham with his wife and two children.

# Being Dead

JIM CRACE

PENGUIN BOOKS

PENGUIN BOOKS

Published by the Penguin Group
Penguin Books Ltd, 27 Wrights Lane, London W8 5TZ, England
Penguin Putnam Inc., 375 Hudson Street, New York, New York 10014, USA
Penguin Books Australia Ltd, Ringwood, Victoria, Australia
Penguin Books Canada Ltd, 10 Alcorn Avenue, Toronto, Ontario, Canada M4V 3B2
Penguin Books (NZ) Ltd, Private Bag 102902, NSMC, Auckland, New Zealand

Penguin Books Ltd, Registered Offices: Harmondsworth, Middlesex, England

First published by Viking 1999
Published in Penguin Books 2000
11

*For Pam Turton*

Don't count on Heaven, or on Hell.
You're dead. That's it. *Adieu*. Farewell.
Eternity awaits? Oh, sure!
It's Putrefaction and Manure
And unrelenting Rot, Rot, Rot,
As you regress, from *Zoo.* to *Bot.*
I'll Grieve, of course,
Departing wife,
Though Grieving's never
Lengthened Life
Or coaxed a single extra Breath
Out of a Body touched by Death.

'The Biologist's Valediction to his Wife'
from *Offcuts* by Sherwin Stephens

# I

For old times' sake, the doctors of zoology had driven out of town that Tuesday afternoon to make a final visit to the singing salt dunes at Baritone Bay. And to lay a ghost. They never made it back alive. They almost never made it back at all.

They'd only meant to take a short nostalgic walk along the coast where they had met as students almost thirty years before. They had made love for the first time in these same dunes. And they might have made love there again if, as the newspapers were to say, 'Death, armed with a piece of granite, had not stumbled on their kisses.'

They were the oddest pair, these dead, spreadeagled lovers on the coast: Joseph and Celice. Both had been teachers. He was director at the Tidal Institute where he was noted for his coldness as much as for his brains. She was a part-time tutor at the university. Hardly any of their colleagues had ever seen them together, or visited them at home, let alone witnessed them touch. How unexpected, then, that these two, of all couples, should be found like this, without their underclothes, their heads caved in, unlikely victims of unlikely passions. Who would have thought that unattractive people of that age and learning would encounter sex and murder in the open air?

They paid a heavy price for their nostalgia.

# 2

Had Joseph and Celice been killed, their bodies found, then carried home not on that Tuesday afternoon but, say, a hundred years ago, when even doctors of zoology could be lamented publicly, hysterically, without embarrassment, their family and their neighbours would have held a midnight *quivering* for them. The bodies would be laid out side by side on the bed in their best clothes and shoes, their wounds disguised, their hair slicked back, eyes shut, mouths shut, his hand on hers, their faces rhyming. The room would smell of camphor, candlewax and soap, and be as full of coughs and hard-backed chairs as a doctor's waiting room.

The mourners, women first, would come as soon as it was dark to start their venerations, weeping till their shoulders shook, tapping on the floorboards with their boots and sticks, rattling their bracelets and their cuffs. Whoever had the squeaky chair or the loosest floorboard to creak or the most resounding of sobs could count herself the most distraught. The greater the racket the deeper the grief. A hundred years ago no one was silent or tongue-tied, as we are now, when death was in the room. They had not yet muzzled grief or banished it from daily life. Death was cultivated, watered like a plant. There was no need for whispering or mime. Let the hubbub drive the devils out, they'd tell themselves. Let's make a row. Let's shout. There were even *quiver* sticks to buy and shake, made out of metal rods with clacking wooden rings. The children would compete for those; their squabbling and their snatching would only benefit the din. A *quivering* should make the whole house rattle, it was said. It ought to keep the neighbourhood awake. It ought to sound as if a thousand crows were pecking at the roof. But those were optimistic times; death was an ill-lit corridor with all its greater rooms beyond.

At midnight, when the men arrived, all the guests would stand to form a circle round the bed. They'd grip the mattress and the bedboards, a shoal of hands, to *quiver* the murdered couple, winnowing and shaking out their wrongdoings so that they'd enter heaven unopposed. The ashy chaff of all their errors and misdeeds would drift like cigar motes in the candle-light. Their tallowed sins would smudge the men's clean shirts.

Afterwards, fuelled by the older children of the house who'd serve them coffee or little cups of Boulevard liqueur through-out the night, the neighbours and the relatives would reminisce about the dead, starting with the hearsay of the couple's final, bludgeoned breaths. And then – with, naturally, some shuffling, dozing silences in the hollows of the night when no one could concentrate on anything except the hardness of the chairs – their recollections would regress through the years. Their memories, exposed to the backward-running time of *quiverings* in which regrets became prospects, resentments became love, experience became hope, would up-end the hourglass of Celice and Joseph's life together and let their sands reverse. When north is south, the dead sit up, climb off their beds, grow younger and indifferent to dying. Skin stretches tight, hair thickens and becomes as sleek as nightcats', blows and bruises are revoked. Wounds close.

First, the friends and neighbours would recall Joseph and Celice's latest months, 'So quiet – considerate, I mean – you hardly knew if they were in.' Then their middle years, their married life, their work, perhaps, their parenting, their wedding, the student days, until – with sentimental guesses at their early lives, what sort of girl and boy they must have been, how they excelled at books if not at sport – their childhoods were achieved.

With practised timing, the *quiverings* for the murdered couple would end at daybreak. As dawn was flattening the candle-flames and deepening the corners of the room, an aunt, a colleague, an old friend would celebrate the wonder of the couple's births over fifty years before, their infancies, how sweet and difficult they'd been, how promising, how loved.

*Quiverings* were resurrections of the dead.

But these are hardly optimistic or sentimental times – and that Tuesday afternoon was not a hundred years ago. Poor Joseph and Celice would not be found and carried home for burial. Not for a while, at least. Nor would their faces rhyme sweetly on a bed. No one would come to hide their wounds or slick their hair. There'd be no camphor, candlewax or soap to disguise the smell of their decay. A thousand crows would not be pecking at the roof. There would be crueller birds and greater spaces. There's nothing after death for Joseph and Celice but 'death and nothing after'.

Yet there can be a *quivering* of sorts. It might be fitting, even kind, to first encounter them like this, out on the coast, traduced, spreadeagled and absurd, as they conclude their lives, when they are at their ugliest, and then regress, reclaiming them from death. To start their journey as they disembark, but then to take them back where they have travelled from, is to produce a version of eternity. First light, at last, for Joseph and Celice. A dawning death. And all their lives ahead of them.

The doctors of zoology were out of time, perhaps, but they can be rescued from the dunes by memory, receding, and tucked up in their waking beds again, still tenants of the room.

# 3

Celice, at fifty-five, was hardly old enough to have lost her fear of death. That accommodation is only for the elderly or the insane. But her dying, chaotic though it was, was far too sudden to be frightening. There were only fifty seconds between half completing her last sentence ('It's not as if . . .') and drawing her last breath. She did not have the leisure or the knowledge to be fearful. She just felt – for a tumbling instant – like she'd often felt at night, half conscious in the falling shudders of a dream. Winded, weightless and betrayed. Her heart collided with her ribs. Her body shook and arched. Her head was loose and hurtling through rimless chambers. Some conjuror had vaporized the earth and emblazoned all the space through which she fell with pixilated, pulsing lights. Her final moments were kinetic, abstract, pointillist.

Judging by the modest blood-flow of her far from modest wounds, Celice's heart had ceased pumping almost as soon as she was hit. Her skull was not as thick as Joseph's. (That was something that she'd always known about the man. Her husband was curmudgeonly, distracted, timid and thick-skulled.) Her skull was weaker than the granite too, of course. The bone caved in like shell. Her brain, once breached and ripped, was as pale and mushy as a honeycomb, a kilogram

6

of dripping honeycomb. It was as if a honeycomb had been exposed below the thin bark of a log by someone with a trenching spade. Her honeycomb had haemorrhaged; its substance had been spilt.

The blows across her face and throat cut off the blood supply and, though her brain did what it could to make amends, to compensate for the sudden loss of oxygen and glucose, its corridors of life were pinched and crushed. The signals of distress it sent were stars. The myths were true; thanks to the ruptured chemistry of her cortex, she hurtled to the stars.

Celice began to hyperventilate, a squall of sips and gasps and stuttered climaxes. Her heart and lungs were frenzy-feeding on the short supply of blood, until, quite suddenly, they failed. They had abandoned her, too devastated to survive. Her chest muscles had forgotten how to rise and fall. Her reflexes were lost. She could not cough or even swallow back the blood. The brain-cell membrane pumps shut down. Celice had lost control for once. She'd gone beyond the help of medicine and miracles. No breath, no memory.

There were still battles to be fought but these would be *post mortem*, the soundless, inert wars of chemicals contesting for her trenches and her bastions amid the debris of exploded cells. Calcium and water usurped the place of blood and oxygen so that her defunct brain, almost at once, began to swell and tear its canopies, spilling all its saps and liquors, all its stored immersions of passion, memory and will, on to her scarf, her jacket and the grass.

Less than a minute. She was fortunate.

Was Joseph any luckier, with his thick skull? Already he was almost lost, though if (the wildest dream) angel-paramedics had arrived by helicopter and flown him to the hospital they might have saved his life, if not his senses. His blood pressure was madly high already, from diet, age, the titillations of the day, and now from shock. His heart was straining on its membranes like a hatching sopbug, pulsing its wet wings against the sac. But he was breathing still, alive enough to feel the pain and to experience the dying. He outlived Celice by more than half an hour.

Joseph had been insensible at first. He was concussed. His grey matter could metabolize only half the glucose that it needed. But he was functioning. His kidneys still processed and cleaned his cells. His stomach still digested what was left of the mango and the cheese brioche he'd eaten for his break-fast, and the humiliating sandwich that he'd had for lunch, twenty minutes earlier. His blood supplied his tissues with their nutrients and sent its white corpuscles to construct their canopies of scars across his wounds. His bone marrow con-tinued to add new cells to the trillions that had already passed their dark, unknowing time as part of him. His pupils dilated in the sunlight. His bladder processed all his waste, although he was incontinent already. He still breathed the heavy, salty air of summer in the dunes. Occasionally he moved his leg or extended a finger. He was warm, kept warm by his unenlight-ened, circulating blood, and by the sunshine. He hadn't put on any screening block, as Celice had advised him to that morning. His naked skin was getting tanned. He urinated down his thigh.

But some minutes later, and against the odds, Joseph came back into the world. He surfaced briefly from his coma – awakened by a rush of oxygen, its bubbles spiralling and rising like the gas in lemonade to pout and burst inside his brain. He'd never heard a wind so loud before or noticed so much odour from the busy earth or felt the syncopated pulsings of his body. The sun was blinding him. The galaxies were bearing down. He turned his head out of the light, despite the pain of moving, so that his cheek was flatter on the grass. He opened his undamaged eye. His spectacles, still on his head, were not broken but they were smeared with blood.

At first, he could see only blades of grass, ungreened by the smudging on the lenses – and then, half a metre to his side, he saw his wife. Her leg was level with his face, braced and supported on its toes and knee. He knew her ankle and her foot. He did not have the angle or the strength to lift his chin and look beyond her knees to glimpse her face. Perhaps she was not dead or even injured. Her leg looked so composed and calm. Her toes were manicured. Her nails were berry red. There was the usual shine on her skin from shaving, the familiar, heavy calf, peppered with sand, the broken veins behind her ankle bone, the foot's low arch, the ochre calluses on her heel.

It must have seemed her leg had moved, a shrug of skin, a spasm of muscle, enough to dislodge some calf-sand and to shake the longer grass under her foot. Joseph tried to bark and squeak her name. His arm was heavy and numb, dislocated at the shoulder. The air seemed too thick to penetrate with anything as soft as flesh. Yet somehow, fortified by his self-pity, Joseph found the will and the adrenalin to reach across towards his wife. He wanted to apologize. He had to twist his wrist against the broken angle of his arm and weave his fingers through the heavy air. His hand – bruised a little when the wedding ring was stolen – dropped on to the stretched flesh of her lower leg, the tendon strings, the shallows of her ankle. Blood from his damaged knuckles ran over her skin but not enough to glue his hand in place. He spread his fingers and tried to grip a solid bone to steady himself. He had to stop his body being swept away, by wind, by time, by continental drift, by shooting stars, by shame.

Her skin was warm, so Joseph might have taken this as confirmation that his wife was still alive, that she might get up off the grass at any moment, collect her clothes and go for help. He could afford to sleep. He started on a dream. An anxious dream in which he'd left his daily ledger out on the deck one morning, on the breakfast table. A careless oversight. It could well rain and wash away his ink, the records of his life. His pages would be turned to pulp. Or else they might be found and read by strangers.

At what point had the life – curmudgeonly, distracted, timid and thick-skulled – gone out of him? Joseph's heart was squirming like an angler's worm, refusing to be reconciled to the awaiting deep, but weakening with every beat. The fish would rise and take it soon. Mondazy's celebrated fish. But the agony did not belong only to the heart. Every pod and pocket of his body played its part, at its own pace, in its own way. Joseph was being gathered in by death, cell by cell by cell. He came to be half of himself, and then a quarter of himself, and then a fraction of himself, which was too small to measure. The music and the mayhem had all gone. His more-than-half-an-hour had elapsed.

They say that hearing is the last of our proficiencies to die, that corpses hear the rustling of bed sheets being pulled across their faces, the early weeping and the window being closed, the footsteps on the wooden stairs, the ruffian departing, the doctor's scratchy pen. That is why our generation talks so quietly in the dying room. And that is why the *quiverings* of old were not a waste. The body hears the widow and the child, the rattle of the chimney-pot, the *quiver* sticks, the life unravelled backwards through the night.

The final sound that Joseph heard was his own bark. His face was grey-white, sheenless, dulled. He was still sweating and his penis was erect, not filled with blood and passion but stiffened by the paroxysms of his muscles. Cruel fate. His limbs and face still twitched, a reflex to the blood's acidity. His larynx was convulsed. The sound he made was not a rattle or a whoop, but more like the call of foxes, or else a gull, or else the unresponding kick-start of a motorbike. Within a moment of the bark – and the few retreating cub squeaks that followed it – Joseph stared up at the day with flat, toneless eyes. Again, no breath, no memory.

Joseph and Celice were irretrievable. Do not be fooled. There was no beauty for them in the dunes, no painterly tranquillity in death framed by the sky, the ocean and the land, that pious trinity, in which their two bodies, supine, prone, were posed as lifeless waxworks of themselves, sweetly unperturbed and ruffled only by the wind. This was an ugly scene. They had been shamed. They were undignified. They were dishonoured by the sudden vileness of their deaths. Only their faces were expressionless. No one could tell what kind of man he was, what type of woman she had been. Their characters had bled out on the grass. The universe could not care less.

Should we expect their spirits to depart, some hellish cart and its pale horse to come and take their falling souls away to its hot mines, some godly, decorated messenger, too simple-minded for its golden wings, to fly them to repose, reunion, eternity? Might we demand some ghosts, at least? Or fanfares, gardens and high gates? Or some dramatic skyline, steep with clouds? The plain and unforgiving facts were these. Celice and Joseph were soft fruit. They lived in tender bodies. They were vulnerable. They did not have the power not to die. They were, we are, all flesh, and then we are all meat.

Joseph's grasp on Celice's leg had weakened as he'd died. But still his hand was touching her, the grainy pastels of her skin, one fingertip among her baby ankle hairs. Their bodies had expired, but anyone could tell – just look at them – that Joseph and Celice were still devoted. For while his hand was touching her, curved round her shin, the couple seemed to have achieved that peace the world denies, a period of grace, defying even murder. Anyone who found them there, so wickedly disfigured, would nevertheless be bound to see that something of their love had survived the death of cells. The corpses were surrendered to the weather and the earth, but here were still a man and wife, quietly resting; flesh on flesh; dead, but not departed yet.

It was as if they had been struck by lightning but the thunder, separated from its faster twin, had yet to come with its complaints to shake and terminate the bodies lying in the grass. Time was divided into light and sound. There was a sanctuary for Joseph and Celice between the lightning and the thunderclap. Such were their six days in the dunes, stretched out, these two unlucky lovers on the coast.

This is our only prayer: May no one come to lift his hand from her leg. Let thunder never find its voice. Hold sound and light, those battling twins, apart. There is a meadow that separates death's chilly gate and the tumbling nothingness beyond, in which our Joseph and Celice are lying, cushioned by the sunlight and the grass, and held in place by nothing firmer than his fingertip.

# 4

Celice was Joseph's senior by eighteen months. A good deal taller than him, too. Once or twice a year when they were obliged to entertain at home, it was Celice who had to reach up for the spirit glasses and the candle set on the cupboard shelf, or, in the spring, cut back the topmost branches on the fessandra bushes that screened them from their neighbours. On tiptoes, she could unscrew and change lightbulbs. She could reach high corner cobwebs with a dusting stick and spin grey candyfloss.

'I'm not tall enough,' was her husband's once-amusing excuse for being idle while she was not. Close the windows, Joseph, she might say. Tidy up those books, for goodness sake. Write to your brother in New York. 'I'm not tall enough.'

Celice's reach was greater than her husband's in all but one respect. In their younger, more outgoing days, when he had had a drink or two and she had shamed him into singing, then he could be astounding. He had the voice of someone twice his size. His tone, so hesitant and quiet in conversation, so inefficient in the lecture room, was magisterial in song. Alcohol and lyrics made him eloquent and confident in ways that talk, with all its set responses, never could.

Joseph's eloquence, it must be said, was out of date, untrained. All the songs he knew he'd learned from his parents. These were dance tunes, sentimental standards, love ballads, patter songs, the sort of music we all resort to after midnight, when the lights have failed. Gas-lamp melodies. Moonlit songs. Joseph would be the only one in any company to remember all the words. He might have hardly opened his mouth in conversation all evening, but he'd still be singing when everyone else, having faked a verse or two, had fallen silent. Then he'd raise his voice and perform his unembarrassed solo, plunging (if the music would allow) through the registers so he could finish with the last line of a chorus on a comic bass. He loved to reach and hold the gravest notes.

This was his party trick.

It was a trick that, for Celice, more than compensated for his lack of sociability or size. Joseph's singing undermined the other men. It left them ill-at-ease, dismayed and dull. Their wives would lift their chins, part their lips, loll their tongues, made wishful by the music. They'd watch Celice's little doctor of zoology with dawning understanding of why it was their men seemed so silent and reduced. He could sing – a phrase Celice had heard applied to a Russian balladeer and loved to use about her husband – like a sea cave, turning ocean into sound. She could not sing herself, even after a drink. But otherwise she was the greater of the two.

She'd certainly been the greater of the two when they'd first met and measured up against each other, on this same coast, those almost thirty years ago. The sapless 1970s. They had been staying at the study house, six young biologists and oceanographers (one from each of the colleges and centres attached to the Tidal Institute of which Joseph, finally and predictably, became director). The study house was on the solid backshore, twenty kilometres from town and more than a kilometre above the dunes at Baritone Bay. They slept in sleeping-bags, the four men in the bunk room at the back, Celice and her one female colleague on mattresses on the veranda.

Celice had not attached herself to Joseph at once. There'd been no instant passion when they met. They were too alike, and had too much in common to be passionate. He hardly spoke on that first day. He hardly moved, in fact. He'd slipped and pulled the muscles in his back on the short walk from the airport road to the study house. One of the other men had had to help him with his boned and metal-cornered suitcase, an inelegant antique and the cause of too much fuss, they all agreed. Joseph, typically, had been the only one to arrive without a rucksack.

Celice, who wasn't generally a fashion votary or even style-conscious, had found the suitcase irritating. It declared its owner to be a boned, inelegant antique himself. In these, her most disquieted and unhappy months, Celice could find no time for innocents like Joseph. She wanted to be courted by loud and tall and handsome men. She had the choice of three.

While the other five students were unpacking, jockeying for the better bunks and mattresses and negotiating where to store their clothes, Joseph had stood in the doorway to the common room, stretching his back and speaking not a word except to say that he preferred to leave his 'oddments' where they were. Strapped and locked inside the suitcase. Celice judged him to be cold, spoiled and snobbish, and hadn't minded in the least when, while the rest of them were trading boasts and backgrounds over coffee, he'd gone to lie down on the remaining and least favoured bunk to nurse his back.

On the first afternoon, they all walked across the backlands and the grey fields of manac beans into the shanty village (long since demolished for the road and an estate of villas) where there was a truck bar and a store. They'd fill their rucksacks with provisions for the week and get to know each other over beers. All of them, except Joseph, that is. He remained in the bunk room when his five colleagues were preparing to go out. When they called him, he said he'd better stay behind and 'fix things up'. And rest his back. He couldn't trudge through fields. Not in his state. He wasn't tall enough, he said. 'He isn't tall enough to piss on his own shoe,' one of the men whispered. Their stifled, guilty laughter broke the ice.

Celice presumed – and she was partly right – that Joseph couldn't stand their company. He didn't want to walk in such a frothy group or be exposed to their good humour or their cigarettes. He'd always hated cigarettes. He wasn't interested in going to a store. Food wasn't worthy of his attentions. He was too serious and grand for meals. She could imagine his unfinished plate, his wine-glass hardly touched. Certainly he wouldn't be at ease in a village bar, having to drink alcohol or endure their conversation. She'd already marked him down as what she called a castaway, someone who'd lost or never knew the trick of being sociable, a single set of footprints in the sand. She didn't care for him at all. She'd been a castaway herself.

Celice didn't really trust him, either. His damaged back, she guessed, was a sham. It was an old man's or a shirker's malady. No one had actually seen him slip. He didn't seem in any pain. She looked around the study house before they left on their shopping expedition. She noted anything that Joseph might try to 'fix' while they were away. He might clear the coffee-cups, for instance. Or sweep some of the sand out of the house. Or prepare the kerosene lamps. Or tidy the disarray of bags and boots inside the veranda where Celice and her colleague, Festa, had yet to unroll their mattresses. He might, at least, lay out their beds for them. If he did not, she would make some light remark at his expense when they returned.

She even checked the disposition of the two ill-fitting drawers in which she'd stored her trousers, shirts and skirts, her notes and books, her purse and diary and her underclothes. The upper drawer was flush. The lower was misaligned, protruding by a centimetre on the left. She'd know if he'd been snooping. She'd snoop, of course, if she were left alone. What might she find inside his antique case? Snooping was the human thing to do.

Celice was glad to leave the study house. Already her companions were showing off, splashing through the marshy undergrowth, more like teenagers than the finest students of their faculties. This outing would be fun. She liked the effortless company of easy-going men. It didn't matter that the shortest and least attractive of the four had decided to stay behind. It made her feel more carefree and awakened to be one of only two women in such intensive company. Joseph would have watered down the mix.

Festa was more demure than Celice, cherry-faced and warmly brimming, with thick, loose hair and an enraging voice, low-pitched and deferential to the men. She wore makeup, even for the walk across the fields, and did her best to overuse her spongy laugh.

Once they had crossed the backlands to the drier fields and could walk along the tractor track, five abreast, it was only Festa who was flirted with. The talk, at first, was dull and predictable, all about the study projects they'd been set and what the prospects for employment were, once they had achieved their doctorates. Two of the men – Hanny and Victor, pampered sons of businessmen – were working on shore crustaceans and could expect to be taken on by Fishery Research, a job for life. Or failing that, they could take over from their fathers in heavy imports and construction. The third, and most attractive, was an ornithologist, ringing and recording seajacks. 'I'm not employable,' he said, but no matter, his family had money. Festa was a biochemist, studying the medical and nutritional uses of seaweed. The three men seemed to find that subject fascinating and full of prospects. They quizzed her on the tests she would conduct, and offered help with raking in her specimens. She told them all the local seaweed names in Latin, making, Celice noticed, two mistakes.

Celice was in no hurry to project herself or discuss her study of the oceanic bladder fly (which lived and laid its eggs in the buoyancy sacs of inshore wrack), though no one asked. She was used to pretty girls like Festa and how they burned up all the oxygen when first encountered. She'd learned to bide her time with men. When she wanted she would be the more imposing of the two, despite her looks. Celice was tall, small-breasted, dressed like a man in shirt and jeans and mountain boots, and physically 'squab' (her mother's term), which meant that though her upper body and her waist were slim, her thighs and buttocks were much heavier. She had the figure of a pigeon or a pear. She took large steps. She drank. She smoked.

She stayed up late at every opportunity. Her laugh, when truly earned, was loud and disrespectful. She was a flirt.

She hadn't been a flirt ten months before. In fact, in those calmer and forgotten days, she hadn't any time for men at all. They never paid attention to her anyhow, never tried to make her laugh or make her kiss. They didn't turn to stare when she walked by. She wasn't prudish. She'd had three short-lived boyfriends in her teens, and though she'd only slept with the last she'd horsed around so much with the other two that there was little that she hadn't learned – and liked – about their sudden passions and her own. But latterly she had become, she knew, too big and plain and clever and, at almost twenty-six, too old for marriage. She was dejected every time she saw an image of herself, in a mirror, in a photograph, in the heartless window of a shop. Men did not seem to see her any more. She turned to cats and cigarettes. Her life would be her work, she thought. She'd masturbate. She'd baby-sit. She'd wear thick glasses, read thick books, and be an aunt.

Then, out of the blue, she'd been seduced by a man she'd shared a railway carriage with, when she was visiting the National Aquarium for lectures. She'd shared his taxi, too, his restaurant table, his confidences, and then, amazingly, his hotel bed and breakfast. He'd said the district where she'd booked her boarding room was dangerous and dirty, and that it was his duty to take care of her. He had been good at taking care of her. She guessed he was experienced, probably by being married more than once and on the lookout, all the time, for border women like her. Passing an evening and a night as the centre of his attentions had been a revelation, a comic one at times because his sexual appetites included playing games.

She'd been 'Madame', a snobbish hotel guest. He'd been 'Room Service', subject to her orders and demands. He'd rubbed, at her request, her backbone and the nape of her neck so skilfully that her eyes had flooded with surprise. Not tears.

The next day at NatAqua, in the break between lectures, Celice was full of self-regard, and somewhat sore. Two men attached themselves to her and seemed to find her clever and amusing. One brought her wine and babbled on about himself, his promising career. The other gave her his address and said that she should get in touch if she were ever in his town. He touched her arm. He spread his fingers on her back to guide her through the crowd.

Maybe, she thought, the residues of last night's games were showing in her eyes. Perhaps there was a lingering odour of his sheets and aftershave, or her pheromones were still out on the town, barking for attention. For once, she checked her face and hair in the long wall mirror outside the lecture theatre. She was both bolstered and dismayed by what she saw. Her lips were smudged and thickened from their kisses. She looked delighted with herself, and far too confident. But, still, there was a new Celice on show. She seemed approachable, available, a sport. Could she have changed overnight? Was a massage of the spine all it took for her to be transformed? Certainly, after that encounter on the train, her ambitions multiplied. She could will herself to be attractive. She could catch their eyes and make men turn. It didn't matter how she looked. It was a matter of deportment. She no longer planned to be an aunt. She wanted taxis, restaurants and hotel rooms. She wanted room service and flooded eyes. It showed.

So, during the last ten months, Celice had evolved a mannish strategy for finding partners. She stood a touch too near to anyone she wanted, brushing his shoulders with hers when they were walking, standing so close that he could hear – and smell – her breath. She'd lay her hand on his arm or hold his elbow when they were talking. She'd rub or bite her lips to make them fleshier. She was trying to rediscover the smudged and thickened woman she had spotted in the mirror.

Often she'd find a man she hardly knew looking intently at her face or running his eyes over her body. She would have blushed and turned away, ten months before, presuming that he disapproved of her, was finding her ungainly, unattractive, oddly shaped and clothed. Someone had written 'so-so' across her forehead in the college yearbook. Other women graduates had scored a 'Top of Year' or 'Man's Best Friend' or, simply, 'Ace'. She knew her eyelids were a little heavy and her eyebrows rather too defined. Her skin was oily, which sometimes gave her face a lively shine but mostly was a curse, as it accounted for the blemished chin where teenage acne had left its purpled stain. Her springy hair was getting duller by the month. She'd even had to snap out a few white strands. But now, a little desperate and aided by what her railway-carriage lover had described as her 'dizzy' face, she could return their stares. Celice was reasonably contented with her so-so looks at last.

Mostly the men she focused on, it must be said, were nonplussed and embarrassed by her unorthodox approaches. They thought she was bizarre and fooling no one but herself. Who was she kidding with an arse like that? Why was she breathing in their faces? Was she deranged? Some of the younger lecturers avoided her. Occasionally, though, she was successful. A few times, recently, she'd taken someone home with her only for the night or afternoon. And, once, just for the forty minutes between waving goodbye to her father at the station and meeting with her professor for a tutorial, she'd satisfied a startled student she half knew in an empty study room. That was the spirit of the age in 1973. Love was disposable.

She had become, she was not ashamed to admit, eager for sex. Why not? she asked herself. You can't make mayhem when you're dead, you can't make mayhem – she was wrong – when you're white-haired. The study week at Baritone Bay was the perfect opportunity for a hurtling adventure of some kind. She would, with any luck, make love with one of these three men, probably the self-effacing ornithologist, or Birdie as she had already nicknamed him, if not all three. She laughed out loud. Just to think of it. The possibilities.

This trio of prospective suitors were not, she knew, deserving candidates. She liked surprising men. These three were callow, clubbish and predictable, and less than subtle, like most scientists. But the very fact of being in a house with them, of sleeping just a room away, was stimulating and a challenge. She wasn't hunting for a boyfriend or a husband – her confidence was not that high – but for encounters. Conquests and encounters. She expected only to be desired and in control for a day or two, not loved.

Even if she did succeed in enticing one of these brash, dull colleagues into her sleeping-bag, she would not imagine that, once the study break was over, she had made a friend for life. One thing was certain, she'd discovered: men are embarrassed by the unexpected women they have slept with. Casual partners don't make casual friends. They wouldn't write. They wouldn't call. They'd cross the street to save their blushes. Festa was the sort they'd marry, not Celice. She was wifely, motherly, petite. Yet, as soon as Hanny, Victor and Birdie discovered that the taller, plainer, odder one was open to their advances, she reckoned, they'd lose their fascination with dim Festa and concentrate on her. One of them would, at least. All she had to do, that afternoon when they were in the bar, was catch an eye or touch a hand or take the opportunity to wrap an arm around a blushing waist. She could imagine the ornithologist tiptoeing along the veranda in the middle of the night to slip into her bed. They'd push their clothes down to the bottom of the sleeping-bag with their jostling naked feet. There was the prospect of a lively week ahead.

When she and Festa returned to the study house, alone, late in the afternoon, already dark, Celice was in a less expansive mood. The men had not turned out to be the attentive company she had imagined, despite her best efforts. As soon as they had left the fields and walked into the village, all three had fallen silent, self-conscious at the way they must appear to the country wives and labourers who watched them going past from their front gates and barns. Their cash seemed heavy in their pockets. Their student clothes and rucksacks felt snobbish and indulgent. Their skin was too well shaved. They kept their voices low, in case their accents gave offence.

Victor was the first to start compensating for his class and education by behaving like a conscript or a rowdy poor boy from the provinces or a farmer's son instead of someone from a family that bullied fortunes out of villages like this. Buy, bulldoze and build. He called out greetings to passers-by in an accent he'd not had before. Hanny and Birdie followed suit. They swore. They stamped their feet. They kicked at anything that lay in their paths – a stone, horse dung, a boulder snail – like bored and reckless country boys. They wouldn't go into the store with Festa and Celice. What farmer's son would shop for eggs and bread? The women could do that, they said, while the men reserved a table and some chairs in the bar. 'We'll test some beers.' Tough talk.

The women, it seemed, would be left to entertain themselves as well, when they finally arrived at the bar with their rucksacks full of local manac beans, green milk, farm cheese and eggs, rice, pilchards, cucumbers, tins of imported meat, bottled water, bottled beer. They could pay for their own drinks and sit by themselves, out of the way, because the three men had taken the three spare stools at the high table and were buying shots of gleewater for the truck-girls there, whose usual customers, the produce drivers coming to the town and the few surviving 'fish chauffeurs' with that day's catch, would not arrive till evening. Whatever seduction tricks Celice had tried in the past ten months were timid compared to those of these young, stalwart girls. They were all fingernails and heels. They smelt of lavender and peppermint and aftershave. Their stockings squeaked. Their lips were pepper red.

The three men had decided to stay at the bar, try all the local brews, pick local brains, eat beans with sour bread and yoghurt like country folk, Birdie explained, meaning that their two embarrassing companions should not expect to be escorted back to the study house just yet, if at all. This might prove to be a long and drunken night, too long and drunken for Festa and Celice who should feel free to go right now, if they were bored, if they were nervous of the dark.

Joseph wasn't there when the women got back to the study house. There was no light, nor had any of the lamps been primed with kerosene. The coffee-cups were still unwashed, the mattresses were not unrolled, and the draught-spread sand on the common-room floor had only deepened in their absence.

No one had tampered with the drawers either, as far as Celice could tell. That was a disappointment in a way. Another rebuff in an afternoon of rebuffs. Even Joseph, the least of the four, might have had the grace and curiosity to show some interest in her comfort and her diary and her underwear.

# 5

Celice could not have seen the granite plunging through the air on his ferocious arm. The man had crept up from behind. He must have known as soon as he'd caught sight of them from the coastal path, drawn by the cartoon sunflash of Joseph's spectacles, what sort they were, what treatment they deserved from him.

Here were people to be robbed. They might have cash and jewellery, and good wristwatches, binoculars, perhaps, a camera, some lunch, some cigarettes. Anything of theirs would be better than anything of his, that was certain. Even the laces from their shoes. He'd help himself to everything, and wouldn't be opposed; they could not defend themselves. They were like rabbits, too weak and mesmerized to run or hide, too soft to fight, too rooted to the spot. He wouldn't try to threaten them. He'd be tongue-tied. They'd possess more words than him. He wouldn't even use his fists. The flesh-on-flesh of fists was far too intimate. But robbing them would be the simplest thing, if he were armed.

The man searched the scrubland near the track for something hard and heavy. A broken branch might do. A length of driftwood. A strip of fencing. There was a piece of displaced builder's granite in the undergrowth. Pink, grey and white, an untender joint of veal, with gristle silica. It fitted in his hand. The perfect friend. He tested its power and rehearsed what he could do with it, swinging his arm, with the granite weighted in his palm, chopping at the unresisting substance of the wind, and cursing at his spectral enemies, the rich, the old, the educated and the loved, the fed, the wordy and the well-laced, whom his shadow boxing made as thin and helpless as the air.

He took deep, energizing breaths, like a weight-lifter, to inflate himself: squat, thrust and strike. He punched the air – a prize-fighter, a champion already, the hero of an unmade film – and smacked the granite down on his thigh to feel how dangerous and bold it made him. The first blood to be drawn would be his own. He was the vanquisher and the comrade of pain. Even so, despite the self-inflicted bruises, it would not be easy to be truly enraged by the man and woman until he was closer. Then, prompted by some detail of their clothes or faces, he would find the fury to engage with them, to embrace them with his energy. He could be (he'd done this twice before) as unembarrassed and as open with his violence as, say, a fox or rook would be. A lion. They took such careless pleasure in their savagery. So would he.

By the time he had left the track and set off to stalk and rob them, the couple had dropped out of sight amongst the dunes. He could no longer see the man's grey head or spot the woman's flapping scarf. But he had noted roughly where they'd disappeared and all his hunting senses were provoked. He'd not have trouble finding them, he thought. He ran along the shore at first, looking for an easy way into the dunes.

Baritone Bay was not a bay in any geographic sense. Besides

its honorary name, it had only the sand and salt dunes of a bay. The sea had not scooped out a wide-mouthed recess in the coast, an arc of beach, two headlands standing sentinel. Instead, the grey-black coast protruded here into the sea, like a delta. Here was an oddity, well worth a visit for students of earth sciences if unattractive for the rest of us, a tidejutter almost an hour's walk from end to end, twenty minutes deep and protected from the haulage of the sea by a horseshoe of submerged rocks a hundred metres from the shore, which broke the power of the waves and left the dunes impervious to everything but the stormiest weather. The coast at Baritone Bay, naïvely unaware that water was more powerful than earth, had scooped out a wide-mouthed recess in the sea.

The bay, of course, was subject – famously – to the wind. There was a constant drift of air that ran along the coast, west–east, so that the dunes were sculpted and aligned like resting seals. Most days the dunes would hum as the wind hugged scarp and dip across the bay. Sometimes there'd be a timpani of scratching lissom stems or the rattle of a sea thorn or a lisping *a cappella* from the waves. But nothing sang. No crooning baritone, so ecstatically described by guidebooks as 'the operatic coast'. It took clear weather, temperatures near but above 16° centigrade, moist but contracting sand, a consistent and exact westerly, and the catalyst of something moving for the dunes to sing their single aria. There was clear weather that afternoon, fine and sunny, with a hugging offshore breeze, but the temperatures were rising still and the wind was misdirected by ten degrees at least. Nothing – not even an operatic sense of drama – could make the bay perform.

The man had reached the outer sea curve of the shore. He

was not singing either. He was as quiet and careful as a stalking cat. He was a noble beast. This part was the most enjoyable, the chase and the surprise. He wasn't nervous for himself. He was in charge. Robbing them would be as easy, to use the childhood phrase, as shitting on a rug. He'd startle them. Even if they saw him coming, what could they do except presume that someone with a piece of granite in his hand would only bring misfortune? If they cried out for help, there'd be no help. No one would come to rescue them. There'd be no miracles. This was both the quiet part of the week and the quiet part of the coast. No builders yet. The dunes of Baritone Bay were – as he was now discovering – a long diversion from the track, hard going, and worth the detour only to those who relished aching legs, and sand and chaff inside their shoes. Walkers took a firmer and a safer route. Someone could die out on the dunes and not be found except by gulls.

It took him almost half an hour to find the couple at their picnic spot, cushioned by the lissom grass. As soon as he had climbed up off the shore into the slopes, he'd lost his way amongst the dunes. One dune, close up, was like any other. The wind had made them so. Their scarp and dips were matching, shape for shape. Twice he came between two dunes to find himself back on the shore again. He almost threw his granite rock into the waves and let the couple keep their cash and sandwiches. The weather had become too hot for him. His trousers had been soaked with spray by running waves. His shoes were wet. His thigh, which he'd struck so theatrically with the block of granite, was bruised and stiffening. Less than an hour's walk away – if he left now – there was a car park below the visitors' centre, which might provide easier profit.

He could smash some windows and help himself to the coats, bags and radios inside. But then he heard a wind-snatched voice, the woman's, followed by a laugh, the woman's again. He had only to walk towards the sound to find their tracks, and the slippages in the dunes where the couple had displaced the sand with their fine feet. He was so happy he was humming to himself. A humming cat.

He discovered Joseph and Celice in a shallow dell, protected from the wind, which now was blowing off the coast more forcefully. They were sitting where the lissom grass was at its greenest and its thickest on the landward-facing slopes, up-wind from him. Two lovers on the lawn.

He crouched behind them, hidden by a ridge, but only watched them for a moment, to check that they were unprepared and vulnerable, that his rock was sitting firmly in his palm, and that he had the strength and will, the inspiration, even, to see this drama through. This was no paltry thing. A thief needs inspiration like any other artisan; he needs some grand and swelling muse, some driving shudder of disgust and ambition to help him bring the granite down. He has to find the fury that links all living creatures, the wildlife in himself, which could destroy in order to create. Where was the pleasure, otherwise?

The muse obliged the man. He took his four long, descending strides towards their backs. He dared not wait. This wouldn't take a moment, anyway, if he was purposeful.

At first, it wasn't obvious that Celice was naked below the waist and that Joseph had discarded all his clothes. It was too fast to notice anything, except the crown and white roots of the woman's hennaed hair. The target for his blows. The detail that he'd chosen to inflate his anger: her white roots.

His arm was in the air. She had her back to him. Her legs were stretched out on the sloping grass so that her body was thrown slightly forward. Her husband sat between her legs, almost like a boy, a teenage son, encircled by the gateway of her knees. Her body pressed against his back. Her chin was resting on his head. Their arms were pleached like turnip roots. She was talking in a wealthy, educated voice, hesitating, searching for the proper words. 'It's not as if . . .' she said. And then her scalp hung open like a fish's mouth. The white roots at her crown were stoplight red.

By the time he registered their nakedness, the stone had hit her head three times. His granite strokes demolished her. Celice fell back almost at once. The granite struck her four more times. Her nose. Her cheek. Her mouth. Her throat. Seven piston blows in scarcely more than seven seconds. Purposeful, indeed.

Her husband didn't stand a chance. He felt the recoil first, her chin was banged against his head. Then he heard her splitting skull, its vacuum punctured. Just for an instant, he mistook the first wound gasping through its gashes at the salty air like the red gills of a fish, for Celice's voice, a startled shush of pain as if she had been stung by ants or by a wasp. Then – too late – he saw the pounding arm and heard the grunts of someone other than his wife. He hardly had the time to turn and check. Or stand. Or make some small sounds of his own.

For a man in his fifties Joseph was not as agile as he ought to have been. He didn't exercise. He had defaulted on himself. His body's pinions, coils and springs had lost their elasticity.

His impulses were slow. His reflexes were numbed. He was half crouching, his body already twisted away from the attack, and preparing to flee rather than to throw himself between the granite and his wife, when the man's heavy shoe struck his underchin and knocked his head back. He received the rock, first, on the forehead, and then more wildly and less logically across the chest and upper abdomen as if the granite worker could not bring himself to break a stranger's spectacles. Too much respect.

Another instant, shorter than a blink – the two men looked each other in the eye.

Joseph brought his hands up to his chest to shield himself against the granite. His knuckles split. Bare bone and blood. Then he tumbled on his back, too winded and too shocked to help himself. Unlike his wife – who, though still bucking from the blows, could feel no pain – he was loudly conscious. There was the taste of vomit in his throat; an orchestra was tuning up between his ears. His gut was punctured by a broken rib. He understood the danger he was in. He must have known that there was worse to come. He did his best to scream, but fear and the constrictions in his throat only made him sound as if he were a very constipated man.

The granite wielder had not meant to take their lives. It hadn't mattered to him either way. He would have simply helped himself to their possessions and gone away, if Joseph hadn't tried to scream. He didn't like the noise that Joseph made. It was disturbing. He stamped on Joseph's shoulder twice to shut him up. He struck him with the rock on the right side of his skull. Unable to resist the obvious, he kicked the soft and naked testicles.

Now the couple were doing what he wanted, keeping still and silent. He needed peace and quiet to search their clothes, their bodies and Celice's bag, the leather sacados she'd bought ten years before at a conference in Ankara, though he was breathless and his hands were shaking like a pensioner's. He felt a little nauseous himself, and close to tears. He'd strained his wrist. It hurt to push his hands into their pockets and lift their bodies. His heart was beating far too fast. But this diversion from the coastal track had been well worth his while. His haul: two watches and a bracelet, car keys, three rings, enough money for a week in a cheap hotel, trousers, socks and shoes, a nice silk scarf. And from the woman's sacados, which he emptied on the grass, a peach, two biscuits, some sunscreen, a quarter cheese in foil, apples, a copy of the *Entomology*, an envelope of toilet tissue, a plastic flask half filled with juice, a strip of painkillers, a hairbrush, notebook, cheese knife and three pens. All useful things. Except the magazine. It landed on the scarp slope of the neighbouring dune.

He had to roll the woman on to her front to search her jacket. She was tall and heavy, uncooperative, and damp. But there was little in her pockets, except a crumpled tissue, a button, laced with broken threads, which must have loosened from the sleeve, and a mobile phone, no use to him, he had no one to phone. He wiped Celice's blood off his shirt and arms and threw the tissue and his piece of granite into the longer grass. He spat away the smell of her. Finally, he helped himself to Joseph's discarded sweater, not only to hide the bloodstains on his shirt but also because, despite the tall heat of the afternoon, he was shivering.

He did not check to see if they were dead. His job was finished. He pushed both biscuits into his mouth, packed his booty into a bag made out of stolen trouser legs – the sacados was far too womanly – and set off with their car keys for their car. He didn't pause to look at Joseph or Celice. He was embarrassed by their age and nakedness. Perhaps he'd not have punished them so much if they'd been clothed. They'd brought this bad luck on themselves.

# 6

The bodies were discovered straight away. A beetle first. *Claudatus maximi*. A male. Then the raiding parties arrived, drawn by the summons of fresh wounds and the smell of urine: swag flies and crabs, which normally would have to make do with rat dung and the carcasses of fish for their carrion. Then a gull. No one, except the newspapers, could say that 'There was only Death amongst the dunes, that summer's afternoon.'

This single beetle had no appetite for blood. He was not a scavenger. His preference – his speciality – was for the roots of lissom grass, the only vegetation on the dunes, apart from the sea thorn and the sapless tinder trees, that could make a good green living out of sand. He had been feeding in an exposed tangle of roots when Celice fell back. Her sudden shadow might have been a hawk. But *Claudatus maximi* was fortunate. The woman's body only up-ended him and pressed him into the grass. Unlike humans, beetles have armour plating on their backs. They're not soft fruit. They are designed to withstand blows.

The beetle flipped off his back and hurried towards the sunlight still visible beyond the warm and wool-roofed cavern, which had enclosed him so suddenly. His legs caught in the folds of Celice's black jacket. Wool was harder work than sand or grass. It snagged on him, a heavy web. But he persevered against the cloth and against the unexpected darkness. Dune beetles choose to feed in light. Celice was an eclipse for him. *Claudatus* did not appreciate the woman's company. He fled her weight and shadow, despite the ancient dangers of the open air, the skin-eyed hawks, the gull, the squadron ants, the parasites, the playful boys with jam-jars. He didn't carry with him any of that burden which makes the human animal so cumbersome, the certainty that death was fast approaching and could arrive at any time, with its plunging snout, blindly to break the surface of the pool. Mondazy's Fish again. It's only those who glimpse the awful, endless corridor of death, too gross to contemplate, that need to lose themselves in love or art. His species had no poets. He was not fearful of Mondazy's Fish. He had not spent, like us, his lifetime con-cocting systems to deny mortality. Nor had he passed his days in melancholic fear of death, the hollow and the avalanche. Nor was he burdened with the compensating marvels of human, mortal life. He had no schemes, no memories, no guilt or aspirations, no appetite for love, and no delusions. The woman had destroyed his light. He wanted to escape her, and to feed. That was his long-term plan, and his hereafter.

The waiting gull, a greater intellect, was too nervous of the bodies in the dunes to help itself, just yet, to any of their titbits on display, the wet and ragged centres of their wounds, the soft flesh of their inner legs, their eyes, the pink parts of their mouths. It bridled its wings and stretched its neck at them, regurgitating its noisy tempers as if its throat was blocked by stones, expecting these two irritated giants to spring to life like resting seals and drive it off.

The gull became less cautious when, after several timid

sorties, the bodies failed to strike at it. It pecked at one of Celice's shoes, which had been tossed a little distance from their patch of grass. It lifted Joseph's underpants, misled by what it took to be the smell of fish. It found a piece of broken biscuit that had dropped from the granite wielder's mouth. Then it went to work and started on the unexpected feast of crabs, which were already labouring through their exaggerated countrysides towards the corpses. More violent death. The sudden downward beating of a beak.

Crabs and swag flies were too numerous in the dunes of Baritone Bay – and too innocent – to be cautious. Numbers made them safe as certainly as lack of numbers had made Joseph and Celice vulnerable. The flies lined up like fishermen along the banks of the bodies' open wounds. They settled mainly on Celice. She had been the more abused, struck seven times around the face and head. 'Seven times killed,' they'd say. Her hair was matted with wet blood and the syrup of her brain. One cheek was flattened by the pounding impact of the granite. Two teeth were cracked, longways. Her facial artery, that superficial lifeline from the carotid, which climbed over her lower jaw to supply the colour to her cheek and feed the brain with oxygen, had been torn in two. Blood had spread across her throat and shoulders and soaked invisibly into her summer jacket. There were dark patches on the grass and sand. Blood does not keep its livery for long. Celice was blackening. It looked and felt as if she'd been pelted with molasses. Her body made good pickings for the glucose-hungry flies.

Celice – an age ago – had put a hand up to her face, to close the wounds or stem the flow, perhaps, or to protect her dizzy looks, her high cheekbones, her somewhat furrowed lips, her acne-purpled chin, the blood-filled lines around her mouth, her teeth. The hand was stuck in place by blood.

She'd landed on a shoulder first, then toppled sideways. The more damaged half of her face was shielded now – too late to do her any good – by grass and sand. Her upper body was still neatly dressed for her day out: the black woollen jacket, a white, rough-weave T-shirt with the quill-and-inkwell logo of a bookshop on the chest in blue, a padded brassière. Then she was naked to her toes. The swag flies found it easiest to feast on the blood in her hair or to settle in the swampy bruises on her neck and gums or at the damage to her hands. They fed in clinging multitudes. Loose knots of flies. They made black balls of wings and antennae amongst the clots, as weightless and as dry as tumbleweed. There's not a creature drier than a fly, as any small boy with a match and candle can testify. Some flies strayed round the bare flesh of her lower body, settled in the hair between her legs or at the tuck of her anus, but found few pickings. There wasn't any source of blood below the shoulders of her jacket. Celice's hair, though, within an hour of her death, began to seem more lively than it ever had in life.

Her husband, though his body was less bloody than Celice's and his face was only bruised, had wounds and lesions right across his chest and abdomen, plus the rifting, open fracture on the right side of his skull. The spittle at his mouth was red and succulent. His left shoulder-blade was broken; his arm was dislocated. He'd not been protected by any clothes, other than his watch and spectacles. And a wedding ring. So when he fell on to his back, his legs apart, his fat and puckered testicles were on display. They'd split and torn with the impact of a heavy shoe. The swag flies browsed his chest and swarmed between his legs. They gleaned the urine and picked at the semen lacquer on his inner thigh.

The crabs, when they arrived and climbed the gradients of flesh and cloth, did not compete with the flies for blood. They grazed for detached skin and detritus, the swarf and dross and jetsam of animals with lives cut short.

Here in the dunes – with Celice's spread body, her rustling hair, her husband hanging from her leg, as centrepiece – was a fine display to illustrate the annual fieldwork lecture that she gave, normally with slides of putrefying seals or tide-abandoned fish, to the faculty's new and squeamish students: 'Anyone who studies nature must get used to violence. You'll have to make yourselves companionable with death if any of you want to flourish as zoologists.' She meant that fear of death is fear of life, a cliché amongst scientists, and preachers too. Both know that life and death are inextricably entwined, the double helix of existence. Both want to give life meaning only because it clearly has none, other than to replicate and decompose. Hard truths.

'You'll need to swallow two long words,' Celice would say, and write SENESCENCE and THANATOLOGY on the teaching screen. Natural ageing. And the study of death. 'Senescence is the track on which most creatures run their lives. Including us. Not all creatures, of course. Amoebolites and monofiles enjoy eternity. Unless they are destroyed by accident or predators. *Enjoy* eternity? Is that the word? *Experience* eternity, perhaps? *Endure?* Even that denotes too great a consciousness.'

Later in their study year, her students would encounter monofiles under the microscope, splitting apart like oil in water, reproducing by fission. Two of the same. Then four. Then eight. Then sixty-four. And all their DNA identical. No deaths. No corpses. Evermore.

A more indulgent lecturer than Celice, less disciplined, more abstract, might ask the class to wonder if that single-celled eternity was paradise or hell. To break in two and not to die. To multiply and yet remain ourselves for ever, world without end. To spread and stretch and colonize and build until there's nowhere left to stand except on someone else's shoulders, until the world is swollen like a boil and fit to burst. 'Death is the price we pay for being multi-celled,' was all she'd say. 'Our tracks run out eventually . . .' More slides. 'These dusk bugs die within a single day, for every bug must have its day as you well know. This land tortoise, still living in Mauritius, has a sailor's name and date carved in its shell. *Nicholas Surcouf. 1803.* Two hundred years old at least. And these . . .' A photographic slide from 1910 of four young women sitting on a bench with a uniformed man spread out on the grass, a cushion for their feet. '. . . are almost certainly dead. Life's only, say, up to ninety years for creatures such as you and I. We're less than turtles. We have to die before they do. We must. It's programmed that we will. Our births are just the gateway to our deaths. That's why a baby screams when it is born. Don't write that in your notes. They who begin to live begin to die. It's downhill from the womb, from when the sperm locates the egg and latches on.'

Celice would take the last slides from the projector, let them contemplate the startling square of light, then add,

'You're dying now. Get used to it!' before she hit the switch to put the room in sudden darkness.

'So, then,' she'd say to her assembled ghosts, as she went round to lift the blinds and let the daylight in, 'we have you here for three years, and maybe five if you go on to doctorates. This is Natural Science. Prepare for death and violence. I'm not suggesting that you go to student bars and pick a fight or frequent the cemeteries. We'll take you to the forest or the beach. You only have to turn a log or rock to see at once more violence and more death than you'll discover in a hundred years of, well, life at this university, despite the instincts of the hard-pressed teaching staff when dissertations aren't handed in on time. Enjoy yourselves.' She'd close her book with a bang, at this, her practised, closing joke. 'I don't believe that any student's perished at my hands. Yet.'

Not true, Celice.

# 7

Celice was stretched out on the veranda when she first heard Joseph singing. Too long and big-boned for the camping mattress, she had hardly slept. She'd always been a poor sleeper. She'd spent the small hours of her adolescence pinned awake in a dormant house, with nothing for her lullaby but dyspeptic plumbing, clocks and the incessant industry of mattress springs. Fear of dreams, her mother said. But it was simpler than that. The faster a wheel is spinning, the longer it will take to come to rest. Celice, the speediest of wheels, was too quick-witted, eager, swift to give and take offence, too mercurial, impulsive, brisk and fretful for easy sleep. She was too occupied by life that first night of her study week to let it go.

Festa, though, an idle wheel, had fallen asleep at once, untroubled. She was wearing earplugs and the hood of her sleeping-bag against the noise and cold. Her heavy breathing was infuriating. So was the rattling wind. So were the men. All four of them. All men.

The drinkers had been late back from the bar, as they'd predicted. It was well past midnight and the world was already tumbling east on its home run when they finally found the heavy, ornamented gate to the unlit study house. They were malt-and-hop buffoons, stumbling against the outside steps and fly-doors and, once they'd got inside, crashing against furniture and each other. The more they crashed the more they laughed, the clumsier they were. The tallest one, Hanny, spilt kerosene and dropped matches before he managed to produce, first, a blue fire on the floorboards, then a clownish tap-dance to stamp out the flames, and, eventually, some lamplight.

The coarse beer from the village bar, served from *living* barrels (microbes, yeast mould, malt weevils, flies) had left them drunker and more bilious than usual. Their sense of balance was destroyed. Their stomachs were so light and volatile they'd floated up, like helium balloons, into their throats, and would rise further, given half an opportunity, a squeeze, a cough, or – God forbid – a yawn. It seemed a reckless effort just to bend, or sit, or even tilt their heads. They dared not go to bed, though it was late. It was too dangerous to sleep. The bunks would sink and spin like fairground rides. They'd never keep their evenings down. They'd flood their pillows and their sleeping-bags. There was no choice. They could not sober up before they went to bed so they'd have to fight off sleep with first some coffee and then the bottled beer that Celice and Festa had brought back from the village. The sweeter, gaseous bottled beer would steady them and keep them conscious till the morning. So they thought.

Celice could smell the brewing coffee and hear the fizz of malt gas as they untopped their bottles and flicked the caps across the room. She was tempted to get up and join them. If she could not sleep, she could at least have some of the beer she'd partly paid for. She liked to have her elbows on a table late at night, even if the company was as infuriating as these three men. She could beg a cigarette, at least. Perhaps she could persuade them to explain their lack of manners in the bar; rich boys had no excuse. What stories had they heard? How was their meal? What mischief had they got up to once she and Festa had been sent away? What had they made of those appalling girls?

She wriggled out of the sleeping-bag, pulled on some socks and her long sweater and, lit by moonlight, felt her way along the veranda to the door into the common room. She was not embarrassed to show her legs or uncombed hair, or smell of bed. This was their second chance.

The men had been whispering and laughing like dormitory boys. The squeak of the door hinge silenced them at once. Their three faces, hard lit by the table lamp and turned awkwardly towards Celice, were fearful and unsmiling. Expecting ghosts, perhaps. Or Matron. Their eyes were hard. Birdie and Hanny put their hands up to their mouths when Celice's face broke into the lamplight and she was recognized. Victor laughed, and said, 'What's wrong?'

'What's wrong with you?' she replied. She was ready either for a row or for some amusement. What were they grinning at?

Celice had met such grins before. Here was the same mixture of blushes and bravado that her younger cousins had displayed when they'd been smoking their father's cigarettes or looking through blue magazines. ('Pink magazines' was Celice's more accurate description.) She sniffed for cannabis. No sign of it, though there was something acrid in the air, other than tobacco and the kerosene. There was nothing on the table top she shouldn't see, just beer bottles, coffee-cups and elbows. The men did not seem to be hiding anything. Except themselves. All three had drawn back from the light.

'Come on, what's going on?' she said, and as she spoke she placed the smell, the lavender, the peppermint, the aftershave, the odours of those bright-clothed girls on their high stools and their high heels, back at the bar. Beyond it all there was the faintest yeasty and metallic scent of sex.

'I see,' she said. There was good reason for their blushing silence, the grins and their retreat into the shadows. These very adolescent graduates had guilty consciences. They'd been 'poking turnip through the hedge', what rich boys do to village girls and goats. They'd paid to go back with the truck tarts to their shanties on the airport road. Their thwarty eyes, their hands on mouths, the smell revealed as much. Celice had not expected that, when she had left them at the bar. She had expected them to boast and flirt and drink, but not to buy. That was too bestial, too devious. She pulled her sweater down to hide herself. It was too soon for them to care about her anyway, her hair, her legs, the smell of bed. These men had spent themselves on prostitutes.

Celice had been naïve, she knew. She should have guessed exactly what the 'boys' were planning for themselves once they were unobserved. Why else would they have crowded round the bar's high table and been so short with Festa and Celice? Why would the men attempt to sleep with clever maiden graduates or even flirt with them, when they could purchase girls like those tough teenagers, and nothing to negotiate except the price? No wasted time discussing doctoral theses. No massaging of spines. No kissing, even. And no boundaries. Money is the whoremonger, to quote Cornelius. Cash fornicates with any open purse.

Celice had seen enough French films. She could imagine the drab and low-lit rooms, the drab and low-lit girls, their skirts hitched up, the meretricious underwear, the unmade beds, and how these three would have been too drunk and overawed and pitiless to take their pleasures slowly. Perhaps they were the sort who'd never learn to take their time. Celice had had a narrow squeak. She might have ended up with one in her bed, and nothing to show for it. She stepped back out of the lamplight. Her legs were cold. 'Keep quiet,' she said, and closed the door on them. 'We want to sleep.'

'Keep quiet!' she said again, perfecting the phrase, as she returned to her mattress. She bit her lower lip and dug her nails into her palms, resisting the temptation to kick her shoes across the floor, or tread on Festa's outstretched hand, or scream. She'd sleep. She'd dream. She'd eat and work alone. She would not waste herself on any of these men. There'd be a week of silences. She'd hold them in contempt. She was too big and free for them. Too tough and odd. Too ugly-beautiful. 'Shut up,' she called out from the veranda. One of the men – smug Victor, she suspected – was trying not to laugh aloud, and failing. 'Shut up. Shut. Up. We're sleeping here.' She had not felt so cruelly liberated for a year. Less preferred than prostitutes, indeed!

It was soon after one o'clock, and Celice was still not sleeping, when Joseph – she'd forgotten Joseph – came back to the study house without colliding with the doors or furniture. The first thing that she heard of him was his small voice.

Where had he been, the three men asked, more sober now, and more subdued. And why the torch? And why – some boyish comments here – the muddy knees?

They jeered, of course, when Joseph said he'd only been walking along the coastal track into the dunes to watch the stars and see what nightlife he could find.

'Nightlife? Oh, yes?' said Hanny. 'Was that nightlife in skirts? Nightlife with furry arses?'

'Furry foxes.' Joseph's voice was careful and defensive; the brainy boy unused to body jokes. 'And there were rock owls and moths and some fine sea bats. This big.' He spread his hands.

'Big tits,' remarked the ornithologist. 'Come on! You've not been prancing on the beach. You've found yourself a little farm girl . . .'

'Some short-sighted little farm lass . . .' Hanny squinted into the corners of the room, contorting his face and pursing his lips, acting the half-blind village nincompoop that Joseph might attract.

'Sea bats. This big, as a matter of fact,' insisted Joseph, unembarrassed by their drunkenness and delighted, even, by his own eccentricity. 'I'm not tall enough for girls.'

'What kind of person – as a matter of fact – goes bat-hunting . . . ?'

'A zoologist,' suggested Joseph. And then, more playfully, 'You've seen some fauna of your own, no doubt.'

'Oh, yes. Wild beasts. We've been riding wild beasts . . . !'

'Well, that was foolish,' Joseph said. 'You took a risk. The light's all wrong.' And then, no warning, he began to sing, hardly lifting his voice as if his comic riddle and its innuendoes should not be heard beyond their yellow ball of lamplight. This was not intended for Celice's ears.

It isn't safe to ride the beast
When the light is in the east.
All riders of the beast will die
Unless the moon has crossed the sky.

Be still while beast light's in beast east,
Bestow beast man with your best beast,
For, once beast star bestrides beast sky,
Beast moon bestirs and beast will die.

Who dies? The beast? The sky? The moon?
The light? The man?
We'll all know soon.

Now they wouldn't let him go to bed. 'Again,' they said. 'And sing it fast, sing it fast, sing it fast.' The little man was more amusing than they had expected. He could be the drunkest of them all, by far, even if he'd only drunk with bats and moths. They insisted that he take a bottle of 'their' beer and sit with them at the common-room table, staring at the ducking flame in the lamp. They wanted more of his exquisite nonsense.

Celice was now despairing and infuriated. The bantering of Joseph and the drunks next door, her snuffling room-mate, fast asleep, the midnight wind wheezing through the timbers of the roof, the far-off whistling of the sands, the disappointments of the day would still not allow her any rest. She was excluded from the passion and the ardours of the night, and yet kept from the anchorage of dreams by all the laughter that was coming from the common room. She knew better than to show her face again. The joy and whispering would end and, given that her tongue and temper were unpredictable, the shouting would begin. She hoped they'd caught some bad disease, she'd say. She hoped their dicks fell off.

'Keep quiet,' she tried again. But it made no difference. They couldn't hear. The three drunks had begun to sing. Pop songs, at first. The Ballad Kings. But no one seemed to know the words. Then parlour songs, taking it in turns to add new, vulgar, badly rhyming verses to replace the romance and the antiquated comedy. Celice had had enough of the men, and not enough. She wanted capture and escape. She wanted to be free of them and part of them.

There was still something she could do to slow her speeding wheel and bring on sleep. She knew how to soften and placate herself. She rolled on to her back on her short mattress. She braced her legs and closed her eyes. She had only to imagine what might occur if, say, one of them came out on to the veranda, tiptoed past demure and sleeping Festa, pulled down the sleeping bag and pressed his beery mouth on to her breasts. She had only to dream she was a shanty prostitute, available to any one of them in some bright bar. How would it be to lend herself to strangers, to part her legs for them, the iron bed shaking in the backyard room as the aircraft overhead came in to land? How would it be to have these men, with banknotes in their hands, lift up her shirt to rub her spine?

She pushed a hand into her underclothes and cupped herself. Her palm and fingertips were cold. She always had cold hands.

Her mother said, 'Cold hands, cold heart. You'll never get a husband with hands like that. You'll make good pastry, though.' But now, for these brief minutes, her hand could be a stranger's hand, one of the men's next door, Birdie's, perhaps. Somebody she might meet aboard a train. She couldn't put a face to him or hear his voice. His fingers and her fingers made a parting in her hair. Her heart was hammering. She made good pastry with her fingertips.

Then, as an accompaniment to the drumming of her heart, there was at last some proper music coming loudly from the common room. Someone, not drunk, was crooning a sugar ballad, the kind her uncle used to sing when she was small enough to be rocked to sleep. This someone had a voice as grandly sentimental as the song. It dipped and peaked as Celice herself dipped and peaked in her warm bag. It shook the bottles and the coffee-cups. It played bassoon. It ran through pipes and veins and joists. The singer didn't try, thank goodness, to add new badly rhyming verses of his own or to undermine the words. He kept the faith:

> *Stand at your window sill, tonight.*
> *Attend my tide,*
> *And mark the harbour with your light.*
> *I'll not be far*
> *From your bedside,*
> *My guiding star,*
> *My midnight bride*
> *In moonbeam white*
> *For I'll be steered across the bar*
> *To you, by candlelight.*

He ended with the familiar, mawkish, dipping chorus, sung more softly than the verse, to discourage any of the other men from joining in, perhaps. The voice was so oddly sonorous and womanly that Celice had to hold her breath to catch the words. She had to hyperventilate and grip the wadding of her sleeping-bag to stop herself from spinning in her bed. Then she was indifferent to everything.

# 8

Celice had become resigned to making love. Better to give way than give offence, at this late stage. Joseph's expectations had been comically, touchingly transparent, from the moment she had woken that morning to find her hand in his, her fingers squeezed, the blinds a quarter open and the sun stretched out in slats of light across her head and pillows. She'd peered with half an eye to find her husband watching her, his mind made up, his web already spun, their day prescribed, his face unusually alight. The weather, he'd said, was far too fine to waste. They had to make the most of it. Up, up and out. He'd brought her an inducement, breakfast on a tray, his usual, clumsy courting gift. Quite a price for a dish of sliced fruit.

He perched at an odd angle in the wicker chair at her bedside while she sat up in bed to eat her breakfast fruit and sip her glass of tea.

'I think we should drive to the coast,' he said. 'Today's the perfect opportunity. I've phoned in sick.' Not quite the truth. 'It's almost thirty years, you know. If you can't do it now, then never.' The implication was supposed to be a visit to the study house, to lay her ghost at last. The bay, the dunes were not mentioned yet. But when he said, 'We'll make a day of it,' and volunteered to prepare a picnic lunch, Celice suspected

53

that her husband meant to lay more than a ghost. He meant to reinflate their past, if only she'd agree. A *quivering*.

He sat and watched Celice while she dressed. Her husband could be as guileless and transparent as a sheet of glass, and twice as grubby. She did her best not to seem too negative. She even, just to please him, just in case, put on the summer jacket and the T-shirt he had said suited her. He liked the drama of the black on white. He said the same about the printed page. Yet she was pleased.

But by the time they reached the bay, at his insistence, she was too hot – who wasn't hot that day? – and still too disconsolate after their visit to the wreckage of the study house to have much appetite for sex. The hour they had spent on the shore below the dunes, hunting but not finding sprayhoppers, had hardly been as nostalgic or romantic as he'd hoped. No kissing with the tide around their knees. No sopping clothes or mouths. No urgency. No blowing wet into her palm. She needed first to eat her picnic lunch and rest before she'd even let him touch her. Then she might relent. Although she doubted it. Times change.

She suggested – half teasing him and half hoping that her choice of an open picnic spot might help to thwart his lovemaking until they were back home, behind locked doors – that they sit on rocks, looking out across the sea at Baritone Bay, watching seajacks and skimmers while they, the humans and the birds, ate lunch. Then they could go hunting in the running tide for sprayhoppers again, the most elusive of insects nowadays, it would seem. That ought to be their entertainment for the day. That ought to be enough.

'I'd forgotten how strange it was out here,' she said, climbing up, despite the rheumatism in her shoulders and her wrists, on to a shelf of heated rocks with sweeping views both out to sea and along the coast. She lifted the straps of her sacados over her head, wincing at the stiffness and discomfort, and took out the foil-wrapped sandwiches and the fruit, the cheese, the flask, the knife. 'Let's eat.'

Joseph shook his head. 'It's windy there.'

'There's hardly any wind.'

'Come on, not there. I'll find a place.'

He should have said, I'll find *the* place because, as Celice knew full well, only fifty paces or so into the dunes behind them, rock free and with no ocean views, was the grassy spot where, all those years before, they'd first had sex. That time she'd been the schemer and he uncertain and reluctant. This time, so far, her tables had been turned. She wasn't sure whether Joseph's torturing desire to put the clocks back to the seventies and to repeat that first encounter, was flattering or manipulative or merely thoughtless. Was this romantic or annoying? She'd allow him the benefit of the doubt, if she must. She'd not be sorry if the moment passed.

'I'll wait here. You find it first,' she said.

'Find what?'

'You know exactly what. Out of the wind. Go on. You get your way. I'll wait.'

Celice removed her shoes, shook out the sand and placed them, upside down, next to the sacados. She ate her sandwiches while she waited for her husband to return. She liked to be alone when she was eating. She'd always preferred her meals to be more contemplative than social; her lunch-breaks at the university, at the corner table with her back against the room, her rest-day breakfasts out on their deck when Joseph was at work, the suppers taken up to bed. These once had been an opportunity, as well, to smoke without her husband's purse-faced disapproval, though Celice had not had a cigarette now for seventeen weeks. Her breakfast cough, the smell, the propaganda, and unrelenting memories of Festa, had finally warned her off tobacco, though she'd only been a dilettante smoker anyway, one pack of Dortmundas a week at most. Those days when she'd enjoyed a cigarette, a drink and conversation, with her elbows on a table late at night, were long gone. She hardly recognized the girl she'd been. So much of her had disappeared. The blackness of her hair. The hollow underchin. Her muscle tone. Her libido. An appetite for trains and hotel rooms. Dunes shift. She could only half regret the way she'd been, how carelessly available she must have seemed when she'd met Joseph at the end of that strange year of sex and fire.

Those early times with Joseph had been difficult. Not loving him. Monogamy of love was something she was suited to. But physical monogamy was hard. How often she'd been tempted to reach out through the bars. These days, though, she was indifferent most of the time to making love with anyone. She would not welcome the attentions of backbone pianists or room service. Her greatest fantasy was a night of unbroken sleep. The massages she cherished now were for her rheumatism and for migraines. They should placate her, not provoke. She wasn't in her twenties any more; the easy pleasures of the flesh were much reduced by wear, tear and repetition. Her shoulders hurt. Her body was more tender than it used to be, and less productive. Besides, her Joseph was a conquest she'd already made and didn't need to make again. At least, not frequently. She didn't have to worry about losing him to someone else. She was, he always said at times like this, 'the only one'. He was her what? Her fifth, sixth lover, and her last.

Was it exactly six or was it more? She spread the fingers of one hand and counted them. Her blessed rosary. The boy when she was seventeen. That's one. Her little finger. She held him snugly in her other hand. She couldn't even recall his name. He had black hair, the use of his father's car and absolutely no idea how girls were made or how to park. Then there was Mr Room Service, the maestro of the spine. Followed by her year of pickups, none of whom had made love to her more than twice. She blushed even to think how she'd behaved, the risks she'd taken for so little in return. A young professor from the city college whose wife, he claimed, had left him (but only for the afternoon). She'd drawn blood on his neck. A waiter, who'd come back to her rooms one evening after he had served – and undercharged – her on the terrace of the Floridel. He'd been a very handsome man but not especially bright or passionate. And then – her thumb – the student she had startled in the empty study room one day. How reckless and courageous she had been. He hadn't wanted to make love to her. Someone will interrupt, he said. But she'd insisted. She'd only had to nudge his trouser front and he was hers. She was in charge of him for at least two minutes. That was one minute more than her command of number six, her little finger once again, a German tourist who was drunk (though beautiful). The last – he lived across the hall, the slipper man – had survived with her a month. He loved the cinema. Five times a week. But not the bed.

That's *seven*, not counting Joseph. Joseph did not count. For when Celice recalled her adventures, Joseph was not on the list. Husbands are not adventures. Nor are they pickups to be enjoyed and then discarded. They are the custom of the house. They are the formula.

The truth is that mature Celice would rather have her cigarettes returned and, yes, some undemanded tenderness in the shape of books, opera CDs and house plants, than her old appetites. Lust had abandoned her; she had despaired of it – and there were times when irritation was the only passion that she felt. She was provoked not by her husband's melting voice these days – although occasionally he tried to win her back with an old song – nor by his hand across her neck, but by his radio, the clutter that he left in every corner of the house, his acid hypochondria, his toiletries, his unselfconscious repetition of the facts.

Perhaps that's why, although the day-long prospect of making love again to Joseph in the dunes had not much stimulated her so far, the five minutes that she'd spent, while he was absent, resuscitating her seven other men had already aroused her so much more. She closed both fists and unbent, erected, one finger at a time, rehearsing once again their kisses and their liberties. How giddy it had been to give herself to virtual strangers, to snatch some passion in the afternoon, to lie out naked on a hotel bed with Room Service attending to her spine and with, of course, a pack of Dortmundas open on the table top. Deep satisfaction was at hand when she was young. She only had to lift an arm and reach. The lips, the finger and the cigarette. How giddy it would be again – a little late in life, too late for him, alas – to be desired, just once, by someone other than her husband. There was, had been, a man. She did not want to put a name and face to him, her concert-going colleague at the university, so recently removed. But that had been her harmless fantasy for years. He could have been her number eight.

When Joseph came back to her rock, a little breathless and disappointed to report he couldn't find or recognize 'their spot', Celice no longer cared.

'It's obvious,' he was explaining. 'It's almost thirty years since we were here. And dunes migrate . . .' He really was an irritating man.

'Let's just find anywhere,' she said, to Joseph's evident surprise. And his alarm, perhaps. She pulled her bag on to her shoulders and, carrying her shoes, walked off between two dunes with Joseph following, his heartbeat almost audible. She sensed his gluey eyes, as if she were a model on a catwalk, naked, clothed, a flick and shuss of skin and fabric. She was relieved to find she could willingly indulge his desires after all and even match them with some feelings of her own. A great relief. She hadn't felt so much like making love for years. She had recovered her old self through memory, receding. A *quivering* of lovers from the past. The drumming rosary of fingertips.

These are the instruments of sex outdoors. You need good weather, somewhere dry to stretch out far from dogs and wasps, and no sense of the ridiculous. Celice wanted privacy, a place beyond the eyes of passers-by, though it was not likely they'd be spied or interrupted. Hardly anyone came out on to the bay, these days, now that the Baritone coast had been 'released', they said, for building. She was looking for a mattress of the lissom grass, which still flourished thickly on the leeward-sloping sand. She found one within a minute, not quite flat, pillowed at one end, a bit too sandy, but it would do. She was in a hurry, but still self-conscious in a way she hadn't been in her mad months. Prehistory. She didn't want to take off all her clothes, not in the hard sunlight, not in her fifty-sixth year. She pulled off her trousers and her underpants and folded them on top of her shoes. Still slim, waist up, and neatly dressed. The naked pigeon thighs. The balcony of fat around her navel. The strong and veiny legs. But she did want Joseph naked. She watched while he threw off his clothes. His penis was engorged but not erect, though she could tell from his dropped lip and his short breaths how earnest and absorbed he had become.

She faced him, put one hand across his shoulder and ran her other hand, her first five lovers, down his chest and abdomen. His retracted testicles were creased like walnuts, damp and warm to touch. She almost said he ought to lose some weight and do some exercise. But she had the sense to hold her tongue. These were fragile moments, soon betrayed. Too soon betrayed, in fact. For she had hardly touched him when he ejaculated. Fulsomely. The sudden shock of her cold hands, perhaps. Bad pastry. There was the usual groan of men his age, the disappointment and the pleasure in one go. So much for well-laid plans.

'It doesn't matter,' Celice said. And, indeed, it didn't matter. It was comical, this failure to contain himself for once, this clownish tragic curtain call, this pantomime called sex. Her husband was a man who lived in fear of folly, denying his exquisite gift for folly all the time. She found that so endearing.

You couldn't call it manly, not with him. But it was lovable.

She made him sit between her legs, so that they both faced sideways to the sun. She made him eat his lunch. 'You'll need the strength.' There was no rush. They had all afternoon to try again. She leaned her body on to his and wrapped an arm across his chest. If she wanted tenderness to precede the passion, then now she had her way. Joseph was not capable of both at once. So few men are. Passion is the work of seconds. You only have to make a god of what you most desire. But the gentler pleasures are built up over decades. She rubbed her knuckles down his spine.

'I wonder if the bay will sing again,' she said. 'Remember?'

They waited, while Joseph ate some of his sandwich grumpily. He hardly dared speak. They listened for the baritone and waited for the flesh to recompose itself. She would have liked a cigarette. A pre-coital smoke. Instead, she kissed his scalp, his neck, his ears. She pushed her nose and lips into her husband's thinning hair. She stroked his chest and brushed away the fallen sandwich crumbs. She reached between his legs and tugged his pubic hair.

'Listen,' Joseph said. He thought he'd heard some shifting sand, a humming voice, a body on the move, a discord in the wind. With any luck it was the dunes.

'It's not as if . . .' Celice began to say.

# 9

They were not the first of their generation to die, of course. But they were early. Being middle-aged and cautious is no defence against Mondazy's Fish. Its bite does not discriminate. None of its deaths is premature.

Seven months before, one of Joseph's many cousins, on a business trip in Ottawa, had stepped off a pavement in too great a dash and was struck across the kneecaps by the swerving cab that he was hailing. The Licensed Taxi Owners of Ontario sent him home Refrigerated Air Freight, with their best apologies. Another cousin that Joseph hadn't seen for twenty years and had never liked anyway, had died that spring. So had a neighbour's son, Celice's age, a bachelor, a cyclist. A heart-attack while he was out training. He hadn't smoked or drunk since he was a teenager. He was birch thin and muscular. He'd not deserved to die. It was too soon, his mother said, as if death was like a pension, a rebuff that you had to earn.

The worst death-undeserved had been Celice's lisping colleague at the university, the Academic Mentor of the Natural Science Faculty. He was the sort of man she liked, now that she was in her fifties. Unmarried, self-sustained, a reader and a concert-goer, always happy to discuss with her the news, the arts, the world beyond their work. She most admired his eagerness, the unjudgemental, solitary pleasure that he'd learned to take from simple things, his small and lively voice.

62

It always thrilled her when he spoke her name. He was, she would have said, a man contented with himself. Except, three Saturdays before, he'd driven up to Broadcast Hill (an elevation most preferred by suicides) and parked out of the rain beneath the grey-black canopy of sea pines, which could be seen in spidery silhouette even from the port. They gave a high quiff to the sloping forehead of the town. He'd fixed a hose-pipe, borrowed from the bio lab, to his exhaust and into the car. When he was found next morning by the first Sunday jogger the windscreen wipers were still hand-jiving to the jazz tunes on the radio.

Celice should not have been so shocked or taken it so personally. The Mentor's suicide was not a judgement on the world, on life, on her. It might have been nothing more than chemistry and genes. He was disposed to it, perhaps. This was his programmed death. A better death, she'd thought, despite her desperation, than the one that she was hoping for: a death doled out in microscopic instalments by senility, her tent repitched each day, a footstep nearer home. His suicide had saved him from old age. He'd stopped the stitches fraying in his life. He had departed from this earth intact, before his final fevers came and the lingering was over, the last weekend of snow or sun, the thinning blood, the trembling touch of strangers pulling down his lids. He'd died with all his futures still in place. His *will*. His *might*. His *could*. There were still concert tickets on his mantelshelf. His winter holiday was booked. He still had debts. The Mentor's suicide, she could persuade herself, was neo-Darwinist.

But it was hard to take a coldly scientific view of sudden death when it concerned a friend, particularly when that friend was someone she could have loved. 'Such bad luck,' Celice had said to the Mentor's sister at the funeral. Though luck, the bad and good, did not belong to natural history, and suicide was not a game of chance.

Nevertheless, somebody should have briefed the Speaker at the funeral that he was lecturing a congress of biologists and that he should avoid such words as paradise, eternity and God. 'You might consider the spiritual reputation of the sea pine under which our departed brother parked his car and sheltered from the rain,' the Speaker had told the mourners, including both the author of a standard text on tree classification and a Chetze Prize-winning botanist. 'We know it as the Slumber Tree. In the scriptures it was called Death's Ladder. Because its seeds are poisonous. But also because its branches touch the heavens and its roots are deep. They reach into the underworld. And so it is the tree of choice. Choose sin or virtue. Descend into the eternal darkness. Or ascend into the presence of Almighty God. Anyone who knew our brother, for whom we have gathered here to commemorate and celebrate, also knows which choice he made throughout his life. He scaled the highest branches of the pine.'

That night, both irritated and intrigued by such absurdity – a pine is shallow-rooted and not poisonous, there is no underworld – Celice had taken down the book their daughter, Syl, had sent her father for his irritable amusement on his birthday. *The Goatherd's Ancient Wisdom.* Page 68, 'A Sorcery of Trees'. She found, to her surprise, that she was partly wrong about the pine.

The Goatherd's wisdom was, she read, that 'Travellers who could not find the money for a bed and had to pass their nights

64

outdoors should prefer the blanket of the thorn before all other trees, And so stay free from harm.' Those 'fools and giddy-heads' who slept below an olive branch would wake up with a headache, 'lasting for a week'. To nap beneath a fig was to risk hot dreams. Curl up in the roots of oak – and be rewarded with diarrhoea. And, yes, the Speaker's prejudice, you'd have eternal slumbers if you lay down underneath the pine.

She read out the passage to Joseph, but he was less affected by the Mentor's death. Indifferent and dismissive, she'd have said. 'Goatherds should know about such things,' was all that he could summon. 'They've nothing else to do all day but sleep under trees.' But, as Celice was to discover when she read on in bed that night, there was some pleasing science buried in the lore. A lengthy footnote by the Goatherd's modern editor showed why the ancient prejudices were not absurd or idle. 'The acid nature of the thorn is not hospitable to fungi,' he observed, 'but mushroom pickers should be warned of other trees.' The migraines and the dreams, it seemed, the never-ending slumbers and the shits were what they'd get from symbiotic fungi growing under olives, figs and oaks, or from the rings of coffin fungus living under pines. '"Come to the pines, you suicides,"' he quoted, '"and dine on these grey buttons in the earth. They'll box you up and bury you . . . New pines will grow where blood is spilt; though it be human, animal or from the wounds of clashing skies, their thirsts are never satisfied."'

Not strictly true. Not scientific on the whole. But this was wisdom widely honest in a way that Celice found comforting. As she imagined it, there was no hose-pipe and no car. There was just the Mentor on his back, awaiting her, the wispy canopy of pines, the deadly buttons on the ground, a ladder leading to his underworld and hers, and everlasting sin.

According to the Goatherd's wisdoms, then, it should have been entirely safe for Joseph and Celice to lie down on the lissom grass amongst the salt dunes of Baritone Bay. The nearest pine was a kilometre away, but there were sufficient sea thorns there to make their slumbers 'free from harm'. Had Celice read on, amongst the Goatherd's later observations (page 121, 'Green Favours') she would have found good news about the lissom grass itself. The Goatherd listed all its common names, sweet thumbs, angel bed, pintongue, pillow grass, sand hair, repose, and then the luck that it could bring to fishermen and lovers if they tied a snatch of it to their bonnets or their nets. Good fishing with the lissom grass was guaranteed. There was no ancient promise of misfortune for any 'fools and giddy-heads' who rested on its cushions, no ladders to the under or the upper world to tempt Celice and Joseph from their second day of grace.

Their tenant crabs dispersed once it was dark. Their flies stayed put, lodging in the damp recesses of the wounds, until the early hours of the Wednesday when an undramatic storm ran down the coast to chase the starlit sky away and flush the warmth out of the night. No noise or gusts or lightning, just relentless water smudging ocean into land, and steady wind. Even the gnawing rodents that had crossed the dunes to feed on the unusual prize of human carrion could not endure the beating rain or the chilling blocks of air that squeezed it from the sky. They fled back to their burrows. The three sets of footprints leading from the coastal path into the dunes, the one set leading out, were quickly washed away. The *Entomology* was soaked. The flattened grass where they had walked, resuscitated by the rain, sprang straight again.

The storm cleaned out their bodies. Much of the blood that had coagulated around their wounds was now reliquefied and thinned to pinkish grey. The rain loosened and washed off most of these weaker stains. It dislodged, dissolved, the clots. Celice's jacket was saturated. Her shirt was black with rain. The water and the cold wind of the storm had some benefits, though. The rotting of the bodies was retarded for an hour or two during night. Bodies decompose most quickly when they're dry and warm, and when insects are at work, taking off the waste. But even the weather and the night could not delay the progress of death by much. Their lives were irretrievable, despite the optimistic labours of the nails and hair to add their final millimetres. Joseph, normally so meticulous, was stubble-faced.

He and his wife were also waterlogged, two flooded chambers, two leather water-bags. Nothing in the world concerned them any more. They'd never crave a song or cigarette or making love again. At least their deaths had coincided. There can be nothing lonelier than to outlive someone you are used to loving. For them, the comedy of marriage would not translate into the tragedy of death. One of them would never have to become accustomed to the absence of the other, or need to fix themselves on someone new. No one would have to change their ways.

This was not death as it was advertised: a fine translation to a better place; a journey through the calm of afterlife into the realms of instinct and desire. The persons had not gone elsewhere, to blink and wake, to sleep and salivate in some place distinctly other than this world, in No-reality. They were, instead, insensible as stones, imprisoned by the viewless wind. This was the world as it had always been, plus something less which once was doctors of zoology.

By Wednesday noon, a gloomy day, their bodies were as stiff as wood. A full day dead. They had discoloured, too. The skin was piebald. Pallid on the upper parts. Livid on the undersides. What blood remained had gravitated downwards to suffuse their lower vessels with all its darker wastes. Celice, her nose still pressed against the grass, was purple-faced. Her downward-flexing knees and upper thighs were black as grapes. Her buttocks were as colourless as lard.

Joseph, dead on his back, was white-faced and purple-shouldered. His lips, though, were drawn and blue, his gums had shrunk, so that his teeth appeared to have grown a centimetre overnight. His nose had sunk into his face. His tongue was also blue – the child in him had sucked its pen. Already he was losing form, though not enough, just yet, to make him animal or alien. Had anybody stumbled through the dunes and half glimpsed the bodies there, they might still have thought the couple were only sleeping, as lovers do, and hurry on, not wanting to look back on such a private place.

The light of day had thinned the rain, though there was almost uninterrupted drizzle until the afternoon. The storm had shifted sand during the night and banked it up against the bodies on one side. Already they were sinking in. Celice's discarded shoes and Joseph's remaining clothes were soaked and almost buried. The wind had lifted his shirt and carried it along the dune gully and into the stretched branches of a sea thorn. It was their flag.

By four the rain had stopped, although the sky stayed overcast and dull. Again the crabs and rodents went to work, while there was light, flippantly browsing Joseph and Celice, frisking them for moisture and for food, delving in their pits and caverns for their treats, and paying them as scant regard as cows might pay a turnip head.

So far no one had even missed Joseph and Celice. They were not expected back at work till Thursday. Their daughter, Syl, would not phone until the weekend, if she remembered. The neighbours were used to silence from the doctors' house. So their bodies were still secret, as were their deaths. No one was sorry yet. No one had said, 'It's such bad luck.' They'd perished without ceremony. There'd been no one to rub their skin with oils or bathe and dress the bodies as they stiffened. They would have benefited from the soft and herby caresses of an undertaker's sponge, the cotton wool soaked in alcohol to close the open pores. No one had plugged their leaking rectums with a wad of lint, or taped their eyelids shut, or tugged against their lower jaws to close their mouths. No one had cleaned their teeth or combed their hair. The murderer, that good mortician, though, had carried out one duty well. He had removed their watches and their jewellery. There was a chance, depending on the wind and sand, that even their bones might not be found or ever subjected to the standard rituals and farewells, the lamentations, the funeral, the headstones and obituaries. Then they'd not be listed with the dead, reduced by memory and legacies. They'd just be 'missing', unaccounted for, absent without leave. His hand could hold her leg for good.

# I O

Joseph rose early on the first morning of the study week, even though he'd only slept since three. He could easily manage on four or five hours of rest a night. He was used to making up the loss during the day, often napping with a newspaper on weekend afternoons or, at the Institute, snacking on sleep while other students were at lunch, in bars. He was not comfortable in bars.

He meant to catch the rising tide on a gently sloping beach. He had to hurry. High water was at eight. He hardly washed – just his face with cold tap water and dish soap at the kitchen sink. He pulled on – for luck – his fieldwork T-shirt with Dolbear's formula (for estimating air temperature by the frequency of insect stridulations) emblazoned on the chest and back. $T = \frac{50n-40}{4}$. He cleaned his teeth with his forefinger, drank cold coffee from one of last night's cups, and went noiselessly outside in semi-darkness. He was as furtive as a burglar, and with good reason.

Joseph had only to cut across the flagstones to the gate in the study-house yard, ten metres at the most, to find the steps and path down to the coastal track and make his escape without disturbing any of the sleepers with his footsteps. But he was tempted by a longer route, to walk through the unattended ferals of what once had been a fine maritime garden and circle the house from the rear. He wondered what the women looked like, sleeping.

Festa did not interest him. She was a trinket. Just the woman to divert the dull and photogenic men who would share his bunk room for the week – if, that is, they could control their first-night appetites for drink and village life. But the taller one – Cecile? Celice? Cerice? a French name anyway – was not their sort. They'd find her odd. And she would find them tedious, he hoped. But, surely, she'd be Joseph's natural ally. She was a stray, like him. Strays pack with other strays.

Joseph had never been a flirt. Not once. 'I'm far too short to flirt.' So he was surprised how much this woman had enthralled him in those few minutes when they'd met the day before. He admired the way she dressed, the boots, the jeans, the dissident hair. He liked her face, her unmasked skin, her unplucked brows, her gallery of battlemongering frowns and winces, which seemed to hold a private dialogue with him. He'd leaned against the doorway to the common room, making too much fuss about his hardly injured back, so that he would have the excuse to stand and watch her while she put her clothes and books away, while she stretched to hang her coat or bent to close a drawer. Her heavy, shapely thighs were centimetres from his waist. She wasn't beautiful. She was provoking, though. She was, he knew instinctively, his only chance.

Joseph should have introduced himself at once. She seemed ready to be spoken to. She had challenged him several times to contribute some small remark, just by looking at him steadily – if such a shifting face as hers could be described as steady – when he must have seemed rudely silent. But he would not, and could not, compete with such unfettered, garrulous companions. He knew his weaknesses: his looks, his social skills, his impatience. He knew his strengths as well. He'd bide his time. He'd take her by surprise.

His was the grandest vanity. He thought she'd be attracted to him more if he stayed out of sight. She'd find his faked indifference a magnet and a challenge. So he didn't speak to her on that first afternoon. He lay down on his bunk and napped. He didn't go with them on their shopping expedition to the village or – an easy sacrifice – to the bar. He was not there when the women came back to the study house that night. He'd forced himself, despite the cold and dark, to walk down to the shore, dead at that hour, and then, on his return, to invent moths, foxes, owls and sea bats to justify his curious excursion. And now he wouldn't be there when his five colleagues got up in the morning. So he would make a mystery of himself, and she would need to solve him.

Festa and Celice were not sleeping when Joseph, carrying a wet-pad for his fieldwork notes and wearing the high surf boots provided at the centre, reached the dark end of the veranda, pressed himself against the outer wall, hidden by the building frame, and peered at the women through the age-ochred glass. Both of them had been woken by the first hint of daylight and by the drumming of the kitchen tap. Joseph washing. The veranda was not screened or curtained, and the roof was mostly timbered glass. Festa had shuffled her mattress and her sleeping-bag towards Celice's and they were sharing a cigarette, sitting with their backs against the planking wall and warming their faces in the smoke. They were too stiff and half asleep to talk.

Joseph could not see their faces very well, except from time to time when one of them drew on the cigarette and spread a brief light on a nose or chin. Otherwise the women were just silhouettes, though the outline of Celice's broad head was unmistakable. He dared not rub the glass to clean away the grime and mould. Glass whispers when it's touched by spies. But he pressed his eye a little closer to the window-pane to watch Celice's chest and shoulders. She could be naked above the thick skirt of her sleeping-bag, or swathed in shirts and tops. It was too dark to tell. He waited for the revealing illumination of the cigarette or a match, perhaps. He hoped to glimpse her flaring throat and her ignited breasts. But he was disappointed. More nose and chin, and nothing that he shouldn't see. Here was a chance, though, to reveal himself to her. He'd walk along the path below the veranda steps as innocent and large as life, and wave, in passing, at the women in their beds.

He'd say, whenever they looked back – not often – or whenever they reminded each other how they'd met, a not entirely happy memory, that he had won her with that single wave, as open a display as any peacock tail, and irresistible. He had only to lift his hand, beyond the glass, and Celice would get up and follow him. The night before, when he was sitting in the common room, he'd sung only for her, not for the men or Festa. He'd heard her calling out, 'Keep quiet!' and then the silence of her eavesdropping. He'd sung the first verse loudly then dropped his voice, to make her hold her breath and listen. Singing was his greatest eloquence. It went through walls. How could the other men compete with such a voice? What was the benefit in being tall and handsome if they couldn't be admired through wooden panels, or at night? 'Attend my tide,' he'd sung to her. 'I'll not be far from your bedside.' He knew that she would join him on the shore. It was not arrogance. It was simply the self-regarding optimism of the young. This was life's plan. The tide would make white chevrons round their boots.

So Joseph walked out from his hiding-place on to the open ground in front of the veranda. He stopped and stared through the windows at the women. He coughed and shuffled until he saw their heads align with his, and then he waved, a bit self-consciously, before climbing the tumbled garden wall and dropping out of sight.

Celice did not wave back at him. She had determined to be unsociable for the six remaining days. The men had kept their noise up through the night and even when, in the early hours, they'd finally retreated to their bunks, the timber study house had creaked so badly in the exchanging temperatures of night and day that Celice imagined, when she dozed, that she'd been abandoned in a sinking ship.

She should have waved, of course. She could hardly blame Joseph for her disrupted night. He was not drunk or germinating a venereal infection like his room-mates. Nor had he proved to be the icy castaway that she'd imagined. In fact, he was amusing. She'd heard the laughter from the common room. And he could sing. What were the words?

> *Mark well the harbour with your light.*
> *For I'll be steered across the bar*
> *to you, by candlelight.*

If only men were sentimental like their songs.

She really should have waved.

She really ought to get to work. That, at least, would be her good excuse for jumping up, stubbing out her half-smoked cigarette and rushing after him. She had her studies to pursue.

Celice got dressed without washing, not even splashing her lips and eyes at the sink. She collected her own wet-pad and her own surf boots as well as a field kit and some specibags, and followed Joseph, first round the building and then over the garden wall that he had inexplicably favoured above the yard gate for leaving the grounds of the study house. At least she'd not be there when the others stumbled from their bunks. She wouldn't have to tolerate their belches or minister to their headaches. She'd not have to witness Festa and her makeup bag.

Joseph's tracks through the snapped masts of the flute bushes and, later, in the mud and sand were easy to follow. It was exciting, dogging him, looking for the evidence of his big boots, and discovering for herself the layers and faces of the coast. He'd descended to a roughly surfaced farm lane, strewn with manac husks. It edged the backlands, skirting a line of freshwater ponds, to serve the few surviving wind-stripped summer cottages, mostly used by anglers. He'd then cut off towards the coast along a signposted path through forest pines and salt marshes before climbing the ridge of the inner, non-salty dunes. A first sight of the sea and the jutting foreland of Baritone Bay.

Celice could see Joseph now, going eastwards on the coastal track through flats and thickets towards the bay. She waved at his back. A late reply. He left the track and walked across the scrubshore on to the beach, still colourless and grainy in the residues of night. The dawn was low and milky, no hint, so far, of blue or green. What little light there was had spread to waterlog the sky.

Celice rested for a while on the dune ridge, sitting on an empty phosphate sack, regretting that she had not brought some fruit, a flask of coffee and a cigarette. Climbing the sand had been hard work and she was breathless. Clearly – and surprisingly – she was not as fit as Joseph, who was already knee deep, wading at the water's edge. She wished she had binoculars.

When she finally reached the sand gully, which led down to Joseph on the beach, she did not turn to join him, as she had imagined, as she would have liked. She carried on along the track towards Baritone Bay. Was she embarrassed? Afraid of more rebuffs? Or cautious? She told herself it wasn't rational to follow his every step like some schoolgirl. She'd frighten him. It would be subtler, sexier, simply to coincide with him by accident, preferably later in the morning when she had recovered from the lack of sleep and from the hurried walk. Besides, the period of resting on the ridge, alone, the views, the detail of the land, the sour ocean smell, the melancholy drama of being young and unattached and not quite warm enough, had reminded her how joyful it could be to have the landscape to herself. She put a Latin and a common name to all the plants and birds she saw. A family game. By naming them, she doubled their existence and her own. This was the pleasure of zoology, to be the lonely heroine of open skies and specibags. Science, romance, oxygen. A potent brew.

Of course, she was embarrassed by herself. What had she been thinking, to leap from her mattress at dawn and rush off in pursuit of this curmudgeon? Just because the other men preferred the village girls to her. Because she hadn't waved at him. So what? Because he hadn't snooped amongst her clothes. Because his voice was fine and, as she had discovered, climaxing. Because her heart and body told her to. Because there was an escalating and persuasive case for running to him through the surf like some starlet from the fifties. She was bewitched. She could imagine being old with him. His was her pillow face. But no, to join him on the beach at once would be unwise. Unsubtle, anyway. What would she say to him? What could a man who hadn't even spoken to her yet reply?

By the time she'd overcome her agitation, by walking as quickly as she could away from Joseph, Celice had reached the eastern hem of Baritone Bay, which projected from the flatter coastline in a half-circle. A balcony of sand. She knew, from photographs and textbooks, about its celebrated cuspate forelands and its capes, its dunefield of crested peaks, which looked, from the coastal path at least, and in that demi-light, like the work of an obsessive architect who didn't know when he should call a halt. Beyond the dunes, the surf was hitting rocks, making bursts of spray. This might be a good place for research. If there were rocks and currents, there might be seaweeds.

There were the usual thorns, a few tinder trees, a single juniper and some wind-wedged thickets of *vomitoria*, flagging their distorted branches on the land rim of the dunes. But once Celice had crossed into the dunefield proper, the sand was unenriched by any loam or soil. Most of the vegetation that she could see was low-growing. It hugged and stabilized the shifting dunes, stunted, stretched and cowering. This was a landscape built and moved by a wind that chased the sand up facing scarps and let it fall on leeward slopes.

Celice had started work already. She'd got her notebook out and was listing species. On the more protected landward side of the dunes, she noted broom sedge, spartina grass, redstem, firesel and cordony. But as she walked further out on to the bay the dunes began to concentrate – though not exclusively – on patchy beds of lissom grass, that misplaced lawn, suburban green most of the year, as spongy and as welcoming as moss. Its Latin name? *Festuca mollis*. In places she could see, exposed by fallen sand, its tangle of roots and rhizomes, half a metre deep and flourishing on salt and wind and on the gritty, spice-rack nutrients of sand.

Celice did not try to cross the dunes. That was hard work, particularly in surf boots. And dunes are frightening for women on their own. Too many secret corridors and cul-de-sacs. She skirted round them and headed for an outcrop of thwarted rock at the near end of the bay, half covered by the tide and half revealed, where she could see the shadow of seaweed and where there should be bladder flies for her to study and collect. The milky morning light, which had been curdled by an unconvincing sun, diffused by mist and cloud, was turning purple grey. The once-blank sea was beryl green. The colours were unearthly, did not last, and within five minutes had been blown away.

Celice spent an hour lifting red wrack clear of the water and removing buoyancy sacs with a pair of scissors. She cut three sacs from each frond of weed, one from the base where it was anchored to the rock, one from the middle where the weed was at its widest, and one from the tip. She placed the samples as best she could – her hands were cold and slippery from seaweed lymph – in labelled bags with seawater and air. That afternoon, if she could stay awake, she'd burst each sac to check the distribution of the flies. Once she'd survived the week and had returned to the laboratory, she'd drop whatever flies or eggs she'd found in vials of fixing alcohol and submit them to the magnifier. But now she had only to dip her hands into the sea and fish for weed. Here was a world in reassuring microcosm. Zoology was a far kinder companion than cosmology. How much more heartening it was to contemplate and bring about the capture of a bladder fly, like some great god, than to view the huge and distant streakings of the sky. How greater than the death of stars was this wet universe, its grains of sand and liquid films, its mites and worms too small to see but swimming, feeding, dying, breathing in massive miniature. These tide pools were a meditation, too. She was surprised by how calm and fearless she had become, staring at the shallows as the colours clarified. And hungry, too. Now (she fooled herself) she wanted only a shower, breakfast and ten cigarettes.

Of course, Celice would have to walk back to the study house along the shore past that other massive miniature, the figure in the tide. Would he be singing to himself, like her? When she drew close enough to wave and call to him, the only singers were the egrets and the gulls. Joseph seemed to be doing nothing more demanding than paddling in the shallows, kicking water like an only child. He stopped, stood straight, looked self-conscious yet again, and kicked another loop of water out to sea. For her.

Joseph's subject for his doctorate was the marine cricket – though, as he explained to Celice as soon as she had shown him her seaweed specimens, it was neither ocean-going nor a true cricket. Its unscientific local name – the sprayhopper – was far more accurate. He wished, he said, that scientists would take more care with names.

He walked into the soft sand, just beyond a breaking wave, to make his point. A hundred marine crickets leaped at his legs, clicking at the effort. Joseph caught one of the creatures as it hit his boots and cupped it in his hands to show her.

'*Pseudogryllidus pelagicus*,' she said, and was disappointed when he did not seem surprised.

'It isn't beautiful,' he said. His sprayhopper was granite grey, the perfect camouflage, and motionless, its back legs tucked and flexed. 'But look, Cecile.'

Joseph half blew, half whistled damp air on to the insect's legs. It disappeared.

'Its only trick. My only trick,' said Joseph. At last he looked at her, full face; a shy-triumphant smile. Quite handsome in a bookish way. 'Otherwise it is entirely dull. Like me.' He picked another sprayhopper from off his trouser leg and offered it to Celice. 'You try. I bet you can't.' He dropped it on her palm. She blew on it. It didn't disappear. She touched it with her fingertip and blew again. It did not move.

'It's dead.'

'You've got no spit,' he said. 'Watch this.'

Joseph whistled wetly on to Celice's palm. His breath was moist. The sprayhopper did what it did best. It winged

Celice's cheek and dropped on to the sand, five metres up the beach.

'Don't worry about him,' Joseph said, as Celice wiped his phlegm off her palm on her trouser leg. 'They never injure themselves. You can drop them from the roof of the Institute, that's thirty-seven metres, and they'll survive. I've tried. Though they can't fly. The wing cases are fake. They're tough, these guys.' He stopped. He laughed. He dropped his voice. 'They're almost lovable. What do you think, Cecile?'

'Adorable.'

'Exactly so.'

Lovable, adorable. The words were in the air. Joseph should have built on them. Instead, unused to flirting, he blushed and scuttled back into zoology. He had been silent yesterday. Now, eager that Celice should not walk off, he was talking like a hobby-laden kid.

Through 'some function of convergent evolution', he explained, his much-loved little beetle, its body shorter than a centimetre from end to end when fully grown, had developed the exaggeratedly long and sharply angled back legs of the cricket family, which allowed it, 'at their sudden straightening', to leap out of view and out of danger. He upturned another specimen and held it, pedalling air, between his thumb and forefinger. 'You see? Its rear legs are more than twice its body length. They have to be. Look where it feeds.'

He showed Celice the waiting sprayhoppers lining up at the furthest reaches of the water, where it had left its spumy hem along the beach. At the next wave, triggered by the air pressure and the spray, they would take their sea-flushed prey – sand lice, salt nits – in their short pincers, flex their legs and fly five metres up the beach, beyond the highest tonguing of the tide. They were absurd.

'It's not the best of lives,' he said. 'It's like living in the gutter of a motorway, feeding off tyre-mites, from speeding cars.'

'The seashore's better than a motorway. It's lovely here. It's beautiful,' Celice replied. She'd never found a place more beautiful. She'd never been obsessed like this before.

Joseph shook his head. He'd always shake his head when she was fanciful. He'd shake his head at her for almost thirty years. 'It's beautiful for us. Zoologists have all the fun. They've no idea, these little guys. They only eat and hop and die. Even after dark. Whenever it's high tide. Most of them only last a day or two. Kaput! The gulls and jetfish get them, if they escape the waves. It's jump, jump, jump, and salt nits for the ones that survive. They couldn't give a damn about the scenery.' He picked crickets off his clothes and dropped them on the sand. 'Sometimes I wonder what they're for. They have no point.'

'They seem to keep you entertained,' she said.

'Ah, yes. That's what evolution has been for, to keep the zoologists happy.'

Joseph leaned across and took two crickets off her collar and another from her hair. This was the first romantic moment of their life. He found a final cricket, caught in her clothes, and placed it on his palm. 'Another go, Cecile,' he said. 'Blow wet.'

For the next thirty years Celice would mock Joseph for this first courting speech: 'Blow wet, Cecile.' She would perfect quite a comic anecdote to torture him. She reproduced his voice, the little lectures that he gave, his uninvited spit (their first exchange of body fluid), the uncorrected insult of her misheard name. She was Cecile for him until he was reproved later that evening by Festa.

'Your father and his sprayhoppers were the most unromantic creatures I'd ever met,' she'd say, when her daughter, then eight years old, first demanded to know how her parents had met. 'I should have drowned him there and then. He could have kissed me if he'd wanted to. Instead, I got . . .' and here she would present her parody of Joseph '. . . "The marine cricket is a beetle, actually. Fully equipped. You see the double set of defunct wings, its antennae and its segmented abdomen? Not boring you, I hope. It's not a cricket at all, in point of fact. I do wish scientists would take more care with names, Cecile."' This was a story that their daughter loved.

Actually, Celice had been oddly charmed at the time by Joseph's revelations on *Pseudogryllidus pelagicus* and touched that he had bothered even to misremember her name. She was flattered that he had shared his studies with her. It felt as if they were exchanging intimacies.

But most of all she liked his playful trick of showing how the sprayhopper could launch itself at will, his will. This was so typical of him. This was the man's appeal. He was a lurking conjuror. Not worth a second glance, you'd think, until he pulled his doves and rabbits from his sleeves, until he startled everyone with song, or challenged them with riddles, or sent a stone-dead insect flying through the air with just a puff of breath.

He was still pondering the sprayhoppers' eccentricities when he and Celice began to walk, ankle deep in flushing water, amongst the living filters, the molluscs and the siphons, back along the shore towards the study house, for lunch. The selvage of the tide was cold and phlegmy. All along the shore the drenching sand was tossing crickets in the air.

# I I

Joseph and Celice did not attempt to leave the ruins of the study house by the garden wall on their day off. They were too middle-aged and stiff for clambering. The flute bushes below the wall, through which Joseph (with Celice, belatedly, at his heels) had crashed all those years before, were now impenetrable. Besides, they understood too well the mantra of historians: the past can be revisited but only fools repeat it. Joseph, it's true, would play the fool that afternoon if given half a chance. Why else was he walking with Celice towards the dunes except to be a bad historian? But he would not steer his wife across the wall and force her through the flute bushes towards their past just yet. That would be sentimental and transparent, as well as bruising. He was not fool enough to think their youth, in all its details, could be repeated quite so readily. Nor was he blind to Celice's inner turbulence. The study house was not an easy place for her. Her mood was sombre, close to tears.

They took, instead, the unromantic route, through what had been the yard gate. The gate itself – wrought-iron irises, made in the 1920s, and valuable – had been stolen off its hinges years before. Most of the granite flagstones had been lifted from the yard. But the steps through the undergrowth were still in place, though collapsed in parts and slippery with vegetation. Celice held on to Joseph's shoulders as they descended in single file towards the old farm road. It was the first time she'd volunteered a touch all day.

No doctor of zoology could be entirely unprepared, of course, for the changes on the coast. These two had read the newspaper reports and seen estate plans. They'd signed petitions to protest against the 'luxury development of valued public grounds'. Yet, even without the intercession of architects and builders, they would not have expected the foreshore and its hinterland to remain exactly as it had once been. Zoologists have mantras of their own: change is the only constant; nothing in the universe is stable or inert; decay and growth are synonyms; a grain of sand is stronger and more durable than rock. If cities could be transformed by wear and tear and shifting tastes, despite their seeming permanence, then something as soft and passing as the landscape could be flattened and reshaped in just one night, by just one storm.

So they did not expect to discover the old farm road unchanged after thirty years of storms. It would not have a surfacing of manac husks or a garnishing of cattle dung. There were no working farms or fields any longer in the neighbourhood. The only crops these days were mortgages and weeds. It was most likely that the road would be pinched and overgrown like the magic and neglected lane of fairy tales. There would be an overhang of pines and heavy shade. Death's ladder to the underworld. Their way might well be blocked by rotting trunks and thickets. Instead, they came out of the trees into a harsh and blinding sky, too tall and blue and punitive, above a shocking corridor of clearances. Construction had begun. The soil was stripped of trees in a swathe of flattened, tyre-pocked earth, twenty metres wide. Great stones and roots were sheared and pushed aside like dry moraines as if an earthen glacier had carved a passage through the land. These were the early, heartless makings of the service drive which, once surfaced, would give access to the lorries and the builders. Later, the drive would be upgraded to a civic motorway to serve the seven hundred homes of Salt Pines, the landscaped, gated enclave ('convenient for both the airport and the city') that would, within a year, begin to house the region's richest and most nervous businessmen.

Celice and Joseph shook their heads. Such were the miracles of man. They walked a few metres along the intact edges of the corridor but then retraced their steps when they were blocked by mounds of debris. Where should they cross? Where was the public path? 'Somebody should complain,' said Joseph, knowing that the somebody would not be him. 'Where are we supposed to go?'

They had to shade their eyes against the sun to search the far side of the clearance for a footpath sign or some clue of how they could proceed towards the coast. There was no remaining evidence of any of the summer cottages that had once lined the farm road. The string of small freshwater ponds, breached and punctured by the bulldozers, had either drained away or had been buried under soil. Occasionally, from the direction of the airport road, there was the harsh percussion of a dumper truck delivering its clinker or its gravel for the new highway, or granite aggregate for the building raft on which Salt Pines would float. The sand alone would not endure the weight of all that taste and money.

It was Celice, with better eyesight than her husband, who spotted the arrowed way-marker, tacked to a pine trunk, which showed the forward route of their disrupted path. But she and Joseph were nervous and reluctant to cross the open ground. They felt like trespassers. The clearance was intimidating, like some contested border from their youth. A DMZ, scorched clear to keep defectors in or out. A no man's land, to hold the easts and wests, the norths and souths apart. The Germanys and the Koreas. The Vietnams. It looked as if there ought to be guard turrets, land mines, Alsatian dogs and barbed tripwire. There were, in fact, two planes above the trees; one high, circling airliner and, at five hundred metres, a single-engined trainer, snooping directly overhead and looking as if it might release at any time a bomb, a canister of gas, a parachutist. Even if Joseph and Celice were not spotted by the plane, snipers would pick them off if they were mad enough to walk out from the undergrowth. Only animals were safe. Wood crows and pickerlings hopped across the naked soil. Rats ran along the flooded lorry ruts to feed on roots and bulbs. Two hispid buzzards – lovers of the open motorway – sat waiting in the pine tops for the carnage that would come. Celice did not regard the clearance as a metaphor, a thick and earthy line between their futures and their pasts. She merely was depressed by what they'd found and would have turned around and gone back home if she had had the choice. If her husband hadn't been so keen to reach the coast, she would have died in bed.

Joseph and Celice began their trespasses. The wind and sun had dried and baked the surface of the soil above soft, ankle-deep mud, but that top layer was as thin and friable as pie crust, too thin to support two heavy mammals. They left deep footsteps in the soil, and the soil made its mark, too, on their shoes and on the bottoms of their trousers. 'Now what else?' remarked Celice, meaning that there could be worse ahead. They might spend the afternoon wading through the mud of endless building sites. Their outing – *post* study house – had not begun well.

But once they'd reached the continuing path and had made their way through the remaining forest pines, salt marshes and lagoons (perfect for the planned golf-course: golf balls float best in brackish water) and had cleaned their shoes by climbing in the loose sand of the first dune ridge, all evidence of Salt Pines disappeared. From the summit of the dunes the wounds and scars were masked by trees. Even the clank of trucks and dumpers was absorbed. The training plane had gone elsewhere. Here was their first view of the coast; the wine-deep, sad, narcotic sea.

They slid down the sand scree to the coastal plain, which sloped towards the scrubshore. Beyond were the dunefields of Baritone Bay. The plain was hardly touched, as yet, by progress or 'landscaping'. There would be a resort village there in time, they knew. A marina, too, and a granite esplanade with shorefront restaurants and cycle tracks. But these would not be started until, phase one, the houses were complete and there were influential residents to overcome the reservations of the more sentimental town governors. Someone had built a small stone jetty, with a boat winch at the top. It ran from the coastal track, across the shore, to the low-water mark. That was something new since their last visit together. And, where once there had been natural barriers of shore grass and a prairie of low vegetation, there were now sand fences to secure the beach, and lines of erosion bags arranged in chevrons to protect against shoreface recession. It seemed, as well, from the way the tides were running, that the disposition of the offshore spits and shoals, bars and channels had been re-designed. Friction and accretion, flooding, overwash and deposition had made fresh patterns. The ocean has a thousand crafts.

Fifty metres offshore there was a new, elongated ridge of sand, which broke the waves and robbed the plunging breakers – their crest curls wrapped round tubes of air, like brandy snaps – of their dramatic energy. They reached the beach, emasculated and at a lesser angle.

At the far end, where Joseph had once sent phlegmy – and seductive – crickets flying, the shore had lost its shallow gradient to thirty years of spilling and collapsing seas. The waves had pushed the sand higher up the beach and dumped a steep and arching shelf of pebbles and shells.

'They'll not like that,' said Joseph.

This could be disappointing. They almost ran along the whole length of the beach, from west to east, looking at the hem of breaking waves, hunting for sprayhoppers in the tide's spumy residues, turning the piles of coal shells with their shoes to disturb any living fugitives. But nothing jumped for them, even though they'd timed their visit perfectly. The tide was high and running in. They should be ankle deep in crickets.

'Not even one,' said Celice.

'One's not enough. One never lasts.'

Joseph was not entirely surprised. As soon as he had seen the steepened disposition of the shore he knew conditions would be wrong for *Pseudogryllidus pelagicus*. He'd predicted as much in his long-forgotten doctoral thesis (grandiloquently titled *Patience and Blind Chance: A Natural History of the Sprayhopper*). They were so specialized and so discriminating that they would be unable to adapt quickly enough to the fickle disposition of the waves. Blind chance had brought bad luck. 'Too steep for them,' he said. 'They need a good flat beach with running tides. That's life.'

That's life, indeed. But it had always been his private fancy that crickets, hoppers and beetles would withstand anything that life could toss at them. They were the grand survivors of the natural world. They were the nimblest of all insects. They were better-equipped than almost any other creature to endure extreme conditions. One had only to keep up with reports in the *Entomology* to know that there were furnace beetles, impervious to glowing coals. There were polar crickets, which lived in permafrost, and blind cavehoppers, which flourished on the limescaled rims of underground pools and listened for their tiny prey through four ears mounted on their knees. There were bugs that feasted on the hot and sticky gas tars at the back of cookers, or navigated sewerage pipes, or chewed electric cables.

There was even a specialist cicada in South America (*Entomology*, vol. CXXI/27) that fed and bred in diesel engines. It lived on emulsified fuel. Its common name? The grease monkey. It had first been identified in the 1970s in Ecuador. It was wingless, with short legs, designed for clinging, not for mobility. But it had travelled north and south, two thousand miles in less than twenty years, by diesel lorry and diesel train. Mechanical migration. It was now common in Mexico City and Brazil.

Single specimens had turned up in engine blocks in Dallas scrapyards. Nature's stories are the best, Joseph often said. 'Except when you are telling them,' his wife replied.

'Whatever philosophical claims we might make for ourselves, human kind is only marginal. We hardly count in the natural orders of zoology. We'll not be missed,' Joseph, in a rare display of scientific passion, had told a student at the Institute when she had been too dismissive of the earth's smaller beings. 'They might not have a sense of self, like us. Or memory. Or hope. Or consciences. Or fear of death. They might not know how strong and wonderful they are. But when every human being in the world has perished, and all our sewerage pipes and gas cookers and diesel engines have fossilized, there will still be insects. Take my word. Flourishing, evolving, specializing insects.' Here he resurrected his best line from his student thesis. 'There will still be sprayhoppers . . . snatching their sustenance from the pincers of the waves.'

Even now, with no sprayhoppers to be seen, the doctor did not doubt his general accuracy. On countless other, more mildly sloping beaches of the coast there would be many active colonies. He'd seen them himself, many times in recent years, on the Mu and at Tiger Crab Edge. It made no difference that he was not there today to witness them or endow them with a consciousness. ('They couldn't give a damn about the scenery, these little chaps.') It was still a disappointment, though, to find that, on this shore at least, *Pseudogryllidus pelagicus* had disappeared.

Joseph's disappointment was not wholly scientific, despite his long-term fondness for the creatures and their connivance in his doctorate. The fantasy that he had nurtured since he'd watched Celice in bed that morning demanded sprayhoppers. They were his Valentine. They were his single rose. They were erotica. If he were to place Celice back amongst the dunes at Baritone Bay where they had once made love, so memorably, so hauntingly, so awkwardly, then first he had to lure her to the beach. So far, achieved. Though by a painful route. But then he needed some strategy more serpentine to take her from the melancholy of the charred remains into the clutching frolic of his arms. He'd need a Venus ladder of deceit, step over step. Something that was more discreet than kissing her or bursting into that old song she had loved, the words of which he could hardly recall. He'd thought the sprayhoppers would be his collaborators once again. He'd pick some off her white T-shirt, out of her hair, blow once more into her hand, set the little creatures flying through the air, and then, perhaps (an innocent progression), drop his spaniel tongue on to her open palm. ('Another go. Blow wet.') Would she then allow his hand to push into her black wool coat?

But now unfeeling nature had thrown up a beach too steep for Valentines. This Venus ladder had had its middle rung removed. Time, though, had not destroyed the light. The universe had not expanded quite so fast. Nor had it robbed the spreading breakers of their sorcery. His wife, ahead of him, calf deep, her trousers up around her knees, was burnished, thinned and immatured by sunshine bouncing off the sea, the silver flattered by the gold. A fillet of her hair fell loose across her face, picked up and dropped by a conspiring breeze. A nape of neck. The waist-enhancing sacados. The tugging whiteness of her underclothes. The bottoms of her trousers wet with sea. A woman dressed in black and white; a landscape dressed in blue. No wonder Joseph was enhanced. Had Celice looked round at what was dogging her, she'd have as usual to give its Latin name as *homo erectus* or *homo semens*. Its common name bone slave or love-gone-wild or thrall.

'Let's go. On to Baritone,' her husband said, once they had walked the whole length of the beach and she was turning to retrace their route. He spoke as lightly as he could, blocking her. He tugged her jacket lapels.

'What for?' Celice raised an eyebrow. Her husband was too breathless and attentive. She didn't need a cricket on her palm to read his mind.

'I think the tides might run more lightly there,' he said. 'We have to see at least one sprayhopper now that we've driven out. There has to be a colony on the bay. Surely.'

'We have to? Why the we? You go. Anyway, it's rocky on the bay. You've less chance finding any there than here.' Celice's feet and back were aching. Her shoulders and her wrists were stiff. Her heart was full of Festa. She would rather sit down on the shelf of shells and pebbles and watch the breakers for the afternoon than risk the vagaries of sex. But Joseph tugged her by the sleeve. She hated that. 'Come on,' he repeated. 'We'll have our picnic there. Out of the wind. Who knows? We might persuade the dunes to sing.'

'There is no wind.'

For once the air above the bay was crystal clear, no clouds to moan about, and even a visible horizon, eye-liner blue, where usually the trading of the ocean and the sky produced a grey mist. Good weather brings bad luck, as everybody knows. Misfortune is a hawk, most likely to surprise us when the visibility is good. Death likes blue skies. Fine weather loves a funeral. Wise, non-scientific folk would stay indoors on days like that, not walk along the coast, beyond the shelter even of a tree. The doctors of zoology were ill-informed. They didn't understand the rigours of the natural world. If spray-hoppers could not survive the changes on the coast, then how and why should they?

# 12

On Thursday at eleven in the morning, Celice and Joseph's mobile phone rang in the pocket of her jacket. Its body-smothered pulse was hardly audible. Insects could be louder and more persistent. Its batteries were running down. The ringing sent a feeding gull into the air, protesting at its interrupted meal with downward flagging wings, and half expecting to discover the rare treat of a fat cicada. It flapped and dithered above the corpses only for a moment. By the fourth trill of the phone the gull had dropped again on to Celice's abdomen and was tugging at the lace of skin it had already picked and loosened. Her skin was tough. In two days she had lost her moistness and her elasticity.

The caller, Joseph's secretary, let the mobile ring ten times – she was meticulous – then ten times more before she put her handset down. It was baffling and annoying that her boss had not shown up at the curriculum meeting that he himself had convened at the Institute for ten o'clock that morning. She'd already phoned his home and got no reply. She'd attempted to reach his wife, the mystical Celice, at the university. Also missing, from her seminar for senior biologists. Joseph's secretary knew that she should not try to contact him on his mobile phone, except for 'urgent things'. That had been his clear instruction. Well, this had been urgent. And alarming. Still was. The curriculum committee, including two vexed professors, a governor and a busy-bored official from the Education Consulate, all equally competitive in their impatience, had been demanding 'updates' and explanations by the minute. Now that she had failed to get an answer even from the mobile, all she could provide for the doctor's guests, as they grew stern and restless in the conference room, was coffee and apologies. It was not like the doctor to be late or absent, she said. Ill-mannered, yes (she didn't say). Remote. Distracted. But never late. You could always rely on his prompt and taciturn presence at meetings. At half past ten, at her suggestion, the committee drifted off, peeving and frowning at the secretary as they passed through her room to collect their coats and umbrellas. It was a rare event: the opportunity to tut at the director of the Institute without any fear of his uncompromising response.

The secretary had her usual rota of tasks to take her mind off the disruptions of her day. There were the departmental diaries to arrange, memos to be typed and sent, letters to be filed or redirected, redundancies to organize. Normally she'd activate the divert on the office phone till lunch so she could concentrate on all the paperwork and take grim pleasure in her unavailability. But cutting off her phone that day, she felt, wasn't politic. At worst it could be taken as a snub towards her absent boss.

When she had tried to reach him on the phone, she had not sensed the ringing of an empty room. In her many years of making calls she'd developed the instinct for telling from the far end resonance if there was anybody there, not answering, ignoring her. There had been someone there, not answering, she'd thought, when she'd dialled the doctor's mobile. Its arpeggio was no dead end. Somebody heard the ringing, could not reach the phone, was in the bath, or still in bed, or on the toilet stool. And would phone back.

Now every time her own phone rang she expected it to be the doctor, though part of her expected, too, a version of the phone call her colleague at the university had received the month before. That secretary's boss, the Academic Mentor, would never show up at her desk again, embarrassed by the typing and phone calls that he caused. He'd killed himself. Joseph's secretary could not shake from her head the image – much discussed amongst the office staff – of the body in the car, the hose, the rain, the radio.

She dialled the doctor's home and mobile phones again at midday and when she came back from lunch at two o'clock, first in sets of twenty rings and then a more determined thirty. Still no reply and still no messages of explanation or apology on her answerphone, though both Joseph and Celice had full timetables during the afternoon. The secretary would not panic yet. All in good time. There'd be an explanation, probably. Some muddle-up of messages, her fault – at least, she always was expected to absorb the blame. A scrambled or a misdelivered fax. An unavoidable diversion. A bungle over dates. The doctor had been away for two days anyway, on 'fieldwork', she'd been told. Some delay was not entirely surprising. There'd been a little accident; the doctor was a clumsy man. His car had let him down, perhaps. It would be foolish – and the doctor would be embarrassed – if she were to phone the hospitals just yet. Or contact the police on such a modest pretext. Four hours? That was nothing. Not in a week when there'd been sunshine. It was not their job, they'd say, to round up absentees.

At ten to six that evening, now anxious beyond reason for the welfare of a man she did not even like, Joseph's secretary phoned his daughter, Syl, at her apartment, six hundred kilometres from the coast. An answering-machine. Had everybody in that family disappeared? She left as calm a message as she could, 'Are your parents visiting? We were expecting them today,' and ended, 'It's nothing, obviously. They've not got home from where they've been. But do call back tomorrow morning after nine, if you have any word of them. Or I'll phone you.'

Syl was a waitress at a studio restaurant. The MetroGnome, next to the concert hall. She was 'the bald and brittle one', half liked, half feared by both her colleagues and the customers, mostly musicians. She was the sort they'd overtip, dismiss as rude, then try to date.

She called her parents after midnight when she returned from work, too full of wine to put it off till morning. In fact, she'd never phone them unless she was fortified with wine or beer. She wouldn't chance the call if she had taken bouncers, swallowed Eden pills or smoked a joint. Bad shit, loose tongue. But drink always sweetened her. She needed to be sweet to risk her parents' anxious and invasive voices. She left the phone unattended on the rug and let it ring for several minutes to give one of them time to wake and stumble out of bed. Her father, normally, should still be up and reading at that hour. Her mother was the sleeper. Syl allowed him time to reach the end of his page, find his house shoes, make a meal of walking to the passageway. She crossed her fingers for him not to answer. He was always at his most reproachful after midnight. Why was she calling so late? Had she been drinking? (Yes, yes, why not?) What was she reading now? What was she doing with her life? (Not wasting it on books. Not rusting in a lifeless town.) It's been six months. When could they expect to see her in the flesh? (Don't even ask. Don't bully me. I hate the coast.)

But when neither of her parents picked up the phone, Syl was more irritated than relieved. The secretary's imperious message on the answer-phone ('Do call back tomorrow morning after nine') had reached into her life without invitation and nudged it. She was rocked. Of course her parents were not visiting. They'd not been asked. They'd never seen her apartment. And if they did show up to nose around, they'd not like what they'd find, her waitressing, her shaven head, her unmade bed, her disregard for everything, her clothes, particularly her unembarrassed appetite for men. Why not take lovers, given half the chance? Why not work through the string sections and then the brass? You can't make mayhem when you're dead.

So Syl wasn't pleased not to have reached her parents. She was six hundred kilometres away from home and yet was asked to take responsibility for a problem that her father's secretary and brain-box colleagues at the Institute had evidently failed to solve. Her parents hadn't shown up for work. So? What was she expected to do at this great distance, in the middle of the night? Divine for them with a magic needle and a map?

Syl's irritation, though, could not entirely mask an intuitive disquiet. She sensed disruption at the gate. She was the sort herself not to show up, to let her colleagues down, to stay out late, to cheat on friends and debts, to keep no one informed, to let the phone sing to itself, but not her parents. They did not stay out at all at night. They never had. They were day birds, clucking hens, efficient, punctual, timid, dull. Sober as milk. Impossible to be with for more than an hour without succumbing to a rage.

She dialled again. They ought to be at home and picking up one of the phones. She let it ring and hunted for another drink and something sweet to eat. Her concern was not yet for her parents' welfare. It was mainly for herself, her hard-fought liberty. Breaking free to live a life without accomplishments so far away from them had not been easily achieved. She didn't want to be tugged back into their rigid, clerkish lives, that too-close ocean smell, or even made to see the family house, those same old rooms, those same old books, those meals. If they would answer now, then Syl was safe. If they did not, she'd have to turn the hourglass and let the sands run back towards her past.

She tried their mobile phone, while she sat on the lavatory with the door open, a can of Chevron beer in her hand and with her own phone, chirruping on its extended lead, between her feet, in the cradle of her knickers. The moonlit bay was at the far end of the line. If only owls and bats could answer phones.

Syl waited for an hour – twelve tracks of a Ruffian Rock CD; ten irate wall knocks from the woken man next door – and phoned again, both phones, the house and then the dunes. She was both startled and relieved to hear at last the mobile phone respond, and then a voice. A woman's voice. But her relief was short-lived. She'd only reached the company's recorded message, 'The user's phone is disconnected. Please try again later.' The far-end battery, damp and exhausted by more than two days of stand-by, had failed at last. Try as she might, their daughter could not get the trilling phone again. It was maddening – though appropriate emotionally. 'Not getting through': that had been the story of Syl's relationship with her parents since she'd left home. Her phone could ring a thousand times and not begin to break into their silences.

Instead she phoned the MetroGnome. The owners had gone home, of course, and just as well. She left a message, aided by the wine and beer she'd drunk. She'd retired from wait-ressing, she said. They'd have to find another girl. She didn't want to slave at tables any more. She had some better things to do. Their food was poisonous. So were the clients. The MetroGnome was such a stupid name. 'Don't phone,' she added, pointlessly. 'I'm not even here. I'm gone . . .' she didn't want to add '. . . back home.'

That night, Syl's dreams were wild and accurate. Beer dreams. She even dreamed of death and nudity – the pauper's Freud. Her parents' bodies had been found, bolt upright in their car. Two heart-attacks. In one dream they'd been driving when they died and the car had left the road, hovered in mid-air, burst into flames. Freeze-frame. A death by Hollywood. In others, Joseph and Celice were blind behind the wheel. They had been found reduced to ash and smoke. They had been found ten metres from the car, thrown clear, a message for their daughter in their hands: 'We were so disappointed by your life.' They had been found strapped in their seats, with no clothes on, unmarked. They were like storm-tossed, stranded seals, washed in the shallows of the sea, drowned by the roar of waves and motor-cars.

Syl had to shake herself awake. But when she fell asleep again, ten minutes later, she was pestered by the same recurring dreams, the flying car, the petrol flames, the naked couple blanketed by windscreen glass and bricks and sea. The more she slept the more her parents' public nakedness would play its comic, unforgiving part.

But it was telephones that really troubled her. In these nightmares the telephone was just beyond their reach, on the rear seat of the car or at the bottom of her mother's bag. Or else the telephone was in their hands but not responding to their stabbing fingers. Nothing they could do would stop the ringing or put them through. Or else the telephone was melting in the heat, or sinking, twenty metres down.

In other dreams, it was Syl's own phone that sounded. It seemed to wake her up but was not ringing when she reached for it. As soon as she dropped back to sleep it rang again. Or it was ringing in the hall outside the bedroom Syl had had when she was small. If only she could get to it in time, if only she were tall and brave enough to reach the phone she'd hear her parents talking from their mobile begging for her help. 'Say where you are,' she said. But all she heard was, 'Try again. Please try again.' Her parents' pulses failed. Their batteries expired, and they were disconnected from her calls.

The waking dream, sidelit by dawn: her father phoned his daughter in the final moments of his life. Had she been drinking, he wanted to know. What was she doing with her life? What books? What plans? When could they hope to see her in the flesh? He could not say exactly where he was.

# 13

By Friday dawn the rain was back, not Wednesday's undramatic, blood-releasing drizzle but lashing downpours. Its moisture was so ambient and insinuating that it found its way into the tightest wallets of the town and made the banknotes damp. This rain was bruising, bouncing, saline. It crusted all the cars with rust. It silvered Joseph and Celice.

In fact, Rusty City used to be the tourist nickname for the town in their student days. Or Wetropolis. Summer heat, trapped by the surrounding rim of dead volcanoes, sucked up the sea – still does, though no one comes to see it any more – and spread it thinly through the streets. Even in the winter there were fogs and frets, lasting until dusk, lasting sometimes weeks on end. There was, and is, a metre and a half of rain each year. Up to Celice's chin and up to Joseph's eyes. And constant windborne spray. 'The windscreen wipers must persist with their condolences across the weeping windows of our cars even when there is no rain,' Mondazy wrote (the Academic Mentor's perfect epitaph), in the years when the town and coast were wild enough to attract visitors. Tourists could buy postcards of traffic in the rain, with his words printed underneath.

Sometimes, as now, there were tidal floods. But in those days there were no concrete breaks and barriers to keep the water back. The floods would chase along the lower town with street deliveries of wrack, eelgrass and crabs. We have fins, the citizens would boast. Our girls have seaweed ribbons in their hair, and gills.

Even death (according to the town's resurrected folklore – Mondazy's work again) was watery. 'We call it Fish,' he wrote in his final memoir, published more than thirty years ago. 'It swims, we say, a silent, unforgiving predator that comes at night out of the sea and speeds into the shallow, less resistant moisture of the streets. Fish comes and takes your father and your mother from their bed. All that you'll hear, as souls depart and make their spirals of displacement in the clammy air, is the shivering of fins.' Sometimes, his superstitious readers and adherents used to say, Mondazy's Fish would show itself only as silvering across the corpse, or by its smell. Death was hardly visible. Yet it was already in the room. And it would leave its wake of scales and mucilage across the sheets.

Fish, for a while, used to take the blame for every death in town. It swam, to the accompaniment of rain on roofs, through bedrooms and through wards where cancer, heart-attacks, old age and strokes had outwitted the nurses and their drugs. It called on people who had drowned in their pyjamas, amongst the reefs and corals of their furniture. Ten times a day it heard the parting rattle in the rusty throats of asthmatics, or hurried to attend a child struck by a car in the sudden blindness of a pavement-hugging cloud, or stayed to witness doctors write, 'Pneumonia', as cause of death for some damp pensioner whose lungs were water-bags when everybody knew the cause of death was Fish.

Fish couldn't boast of many sailors drowned at sea. In those days Rusty City was a tourist, not a fishing, town. (It's neither now.) Only visitors chose to dine on seafood so there wasn't much call for fishermen or fish 'chauffeurs'. But they were bound to lose some people to the waves each year. There was always some outsider who wanted to run along the front at high tide in a storm to take a photograph of pouncing seas. Or see if he could race down the now-demolished jetty, touch the flagpole at the end, and return to his companions before the next wave came. Two months before Celice and Joseph's study week a couple tried to save their dog when curling water swept it from the town beach. The woman went into the water, fully dressed, reaching for the dog's lead. When Fish found her, up the coast a few hours later, the sea had stripped her of her clothes. She was a nearly naked body wearing only shoes, her fingers wrapped around the dog's red collar, and neither of them quite dead yet. Fish had to flap and wriggle over frothing rocks to brush their lids with its dispatching fins.

Wise people in Wetropolis, who did not want to die until they were old and ready for it, stretched nets across the headboards of their beds, or wore a fishhook on a chain around their throats. Even today, long since Mondazy resurrected Fish, there are still a few surviving men and women in the town who won't eat fish at all or let a fish inside the house, not even in a tin to feed their cats. They remember what happened at the Pisces restaurant, down at the port, in 1968. Nine diners at a wedding feast and a waiter died. Fish came and poisoned them. It was a massacre. The bride did not survive to join her husband on the honeymoon.

These same wise people in Wetropolis might find in Joseph and Celice, on their fourth day of putrefaction in the dunes, much evidence of Fish. Their deaths seemed watery, as if they had been swept by curling breakers off the beach and dumped. They had both dissolved and stiffened. They were becoming partly semi-fluid mass and partly salted drift; sea things. They even smelt marine, as corrupt and spermy as rotting bladderwrack or fish manure.

There was, of course, their silvering, as further evidence that Fish had been. It was its watermark. In that dawn light and that hard rain and at a passing distance, the corpses would have looked like shiny human earrings made by fairy silversmiths and dropped by giants, two shards of fallen ice, two metal leaves, two scaly sculptures beaten out of tin and verdigris'd with mildew and with mould.

Even if the light were blocked, there would still appear to be a jewelling to their bodies, where life's soft pink and death's smudged grey conspired to find the silver in between. And there'd still be a tracery of lucent white where snails and slugs had made enamel patterns on the flesh with their saliva trails. These would be the patterns, surely, that Mondazy had described, the wake of scales and mucilage where gasping Fish had wriggled on its fins across the dunes to touch their skin.

Viewed from closer up, there were colours and motifs on Joseph and Celice that Fish could never leave. A dazzling filigree of pine-brown surface veins, which gave an arborescent pattern to the skin. The blossoming of blisters, their flaring red corollas and yellow ovaries like rock roses. And in the warmer, gaping caverns – sub-rib, sub-flesh, sub-skull – the garish blues and reds and greens of their disrupted, bloated frames. They were too rotten now and far too rank to hold much allure for gulls or crabs. They'd been passed down, through classes, orders, species, to the last in line, the lumpen multitude, the grubs, the loopers and the millipedes, the button lice, the tubal worms and flets, the *bon viveur* or nectar bugs, which had either too many legs or none.

The swag-fly maggots had started to emerge on this fourth day from their pod larvae, generated by the putrid heat in Joseph and Celice's innards. Long dead – but still producing energy! The maggots gorged and tumbled in the carrion, as balls of rain as big as them and fifty times as heavy came down like meteorites to pound and shake their caverns and their dells. Death fattens us to dine on us. The maggots are the minstrels at his feast.

Joseph, like most zoologists, had been a faculty snob and hated botany. He thought the 'plant men' lived a lesser life. He was the huntsman to their gatherers. Their only weapons were the plastic bag and trowel. But he was closer now to botany than he had ever been. His greater, living predators had gone, but the longer blades of lissom grass, gasping for the light, were bending over him like nurses. His body was a vegetable, skin and pulp and fibre. His bones were wood. Soon, if no one came to help, the maggots would dismantle him. Then his body could only be gathered up by trowels and put in plastic bags.

It would be comforting, of course, to believe that humans are more durable than other animals, to think that by some miracle (of natural science obviously) his hand and her lower leg remained unspoiled, enfolding and enclosed, that his one fingertip was still amongst her baby hairs, that her ankle skin was firm and pastel-grained, and that her toenails were still berry red and manicured. But death does not discriminate. All flesh is flesh. And Joseph and Celice were sullied everywhere.

His fingernails were split and loosening. His hand was angular and void, a starched and empty glove. Her lower leg was little more than rind.

But the rain, the wind, the shooting stars, the maggots and the shame had not succeeded yet in blowing them away or bringing to an end their days of grace. There'd been no thunderclap so far. His hand was touching her. The flesh on flesh. The fingertip across the tendon strings. He still held on. She still was held.

'We know that Fish will poison all of us one day,' Mondazy wrote, in his death year. 'We wait for it to push its nose into the corners of our house, our room. Too weak to move, we'll watch it browse the mildewed woodwork and graze amongst the timber lichens, which grow as black as barnacles along the window-frames beside our beds, until it turns to cast its sideways eye on us. Our town is mouldering. We are eroded by the wind and salt and rain. We live in fear of water and of death.'

# 14

It was Fire not Fish that put an end to Festa. Some water might have saved her life.

Early, on her fifth day of research, the study house was hardly visible. A damp sea mist had dug more deeply into the land than usual. It had crossed the high, absorbent peaks of the inner dunes, depositing its slightly brackish dew into the sweet-water ponds and puffing its grey breath against the veranda's clammy glass.

Inside, at seven in the morning, the hopeful doctors were all sleeping, even Celice. Their thesis tutor had visited the evening before for dinner and had expressed his broad approval of their field researches, if not their cooking. That night, when he had gone back to the Institute, they celebrated with four bottles of Van Paña and a drunken game of charades. They'd had to mime the names of animals. Joseph guessed the spray-hopper as soon as Celice puffed across her palm at him, like someone blowing kisses. The others seemed to take it as the natural order of the universe that Joseph and Celice would become attached, though they neither touched nor paid excessive attention to each other. Odd sticks to odd; that was the formula. The three men flirted only with Festa. In fact, at two in the morning, when everyone else had gone to bed and sleep, Festa and the ornithologist were still in the common room, kissing noisily.

It must have been one of those two, Joseph thought, who'd placed the kerosene lamp underneath the table and turned the flame down to its lowest setting for a more romantic light, perhaps, then left it burning through the night. He wasn't even sure if he'd imagined it. When he'd got up at seven thirty the common room was almost bright with natural light. The feeble kerosene flame would not have been especially notice-able. It might, in fact, have been already dead. He'd only half noticed it before rushing out to circumnavigate the house and stand on the open ground outside the veranda waiting for Celice. Joseph wasn't sure if there was any smell from charring wood. He should, he knew, have checked the lamp and turned it out if it was on, or moved it somewhere safe away from wood before he left the study house. 'Maybe, even if I'd definitely seen a flame I'd not have turned it out,' he admitted to Celice, years later, to comfort her. He was not the sort to interfere. He was preoccupied. Thank heavens that he didn't say, 'I'm far too short to play with fire.'

Celice had not seen anything, no light, no lamp. She'd only seen Sprayhopper Man, waiting outside for her as she'd asked ('instructed' was the truer word, he'd say), half consumed by mist and half obscured by ochred glass.

The night before, Joseph had admitted – drink talks – that he'd spied on her through the veranda windows. Such an arousing liberty, Celice had thought, and one that she was impatient to repeat. 'Come for me in the morning,' she had said, when they had gone back to their beds. Indeed, he'd come for her, come into her, come with her a dozen times that night, in dreams. He'd sung for her. He'd played piano on the bone-keys of her spine. He'd held her in his palm and breathed on her and she had flexed and sprung her endless legs for him and tumbled in the air.

So when she saw him standing in the garden, beyond the glass, Celice was hungry to be loved. She did not try to hide herself, nor did she try to show herself. She just pulled down the sleeping-bag and stood up, naked on the mattress, as if she didn't know that she had purposefully placed him there to watch her tug her nightshirt by its shoulders high above her head. For a few seconds, she was blinded by material and Joseph was enlightened on how her body looked. The pear. The pigeon. And the truth of it. The wisp and tuft of body hair. Her shoulders and her modest breasts. Her squabby hips. Her virtues and her blemishes. When her head and hair sprang out again into the light she half expected to find Joseph with his nose pressed to the glass. But – and this was touching and oddly arousing too – he had stayed exactly where he was, a soft-edged figure in the mist. She dressed for him. A shirt, no brassière. Some underclothes. Jumper, trousers, socks and walking boots. She put her fingers through her hair, a mermaid's comb, and waved at him. For Celice this was the high point of their love.

How long had Festa been awake and watching her? (She'd never have the chance to ask.) But while Celice was sitting on her mattress tying her shoelaces, her room-mate suddenly sat up in her sleeping-bag, bleary-eyed and pastry-faced, and begged for one of Celice's cigarettes. 'I'm feeling awful,' she said, and gave her irritating laugh. 'My mouth's a bird's cage.'

'I'm not surprised.' Celice lit two cigarettes and handed one to Festa. 'Go back to sleep,' she said. 'I'm going down to the bay with Joseph.'

'You work too hard.' It would seem that Festa hadn't noticed the garden spy, thank goodness. 'Are you going to make some coffee?'

'I'm leaving now. We want to catch the tides,' she lied. 'I'll put the water on.'

That's exactly what she'd done. She had half noticed the lamp, she'd say, either underneath the common-room table or on top of it. She wasn't sure. She had, she thought, taken her still burning cigarette with her into the common room. It was just possible that she had left it standing on its end on the veranda floor. That was her habit, balancing a narrow cigarette to knit its thinning scarf of smoke while she was busy doing something else. Or – so many oversights, so many ways to fail – she might have left the cigarette standing on the table by the sink while she splashed her face and filled the saucepan with water for Festa's coffee. Or she might have stubbed the cigarette out in the sink. She was too hurried to take much notice. Two things were certain. When she left the study house on this, her grimmest day, Festa was half asleep and smoking in her bed. And there was a naked light below the saucepan on the unattended hob.

Here, then, were several possibilities. There was no evidence to say which one occurred. The study house – all wood and glass – was too badly burned for autopsies. The unextinguished lamp, left to burn all night and left to burn by Joseph, too, as he went out that morning, finally gave purchase to a second flame on the underside of the table in the common room. The wood had blackened, charred and finally surrendered to combustion. The flame was upside down and would not have burned for long if this had been a modern table, its polish and its lacquers emasculated by the safety rules of modern manufacturing. The timber of this table had been sealed by combustible varnishes, which were too old to liquefy when heated, but dried instead, went scaly, lifted from the wood in flakes and dunes, and let the flames migrate across the table's underside.

Or else the unwatched hob, in a sleeping house, boiled off the water in the coffee pan until the pan itself began to cook. Its bottom would have enamelled first, bright greys and blues. Then the gas flames would have begun to spread. They'd have licked the sides and tongued the plastic handle of the pan. Pan plastic doesn't melt. It flares. And if the heat becomes intolerable it turns the energy it cannot cope with into squibby detonations, which crack and spring with flames. The pan, unsteadied by the discharges, could have fallen off the hob and spread its molten metals on the boards.

Or maybe one of those nicely balanced cigarettes, which Celice might have left burning on the table by the sink, on the veranda floor, had toppled over to smoulder on the splintered wood in its sweet time. Or Festa might have fallen back to sleep and dropped her own kingsize, her first gasp of the day, on to her mattress to bake herself in man-made flaming fibres. Or she might have stumbled out to make her coffee from the boiling water and caught the lamp beneath the table with a toe on her way back to bed. The spilt kerosene would race across the floor. So would its chasing flame. Or else. Or anything. Or something different. The dead don't speak. It could have started in a thousand ways.

Whatever the initial cause, whosoever fault it was, whoever volunteered to take the blame, a tongue of flame could hardly wish for more dry wood.

The three sleeping men were lucky: their door was closed so when the first flame dipped and reached for fuel and oxygen, stretching its neck for sustenance like a little orange chick, they could not hear the flexing of the floorboards or smell the scorching timber and the melting paint in the adjoining room. They did not wake at the explosion of the lamp with its shallow reservoir of kerosene or sit up startled as the kindled wood finally ignited and combusted with the detonating crackle of musketry.

The fire seemed to have two speeds, the thorough and methodical, and the racing. First there was the toasting of the wood, the snacking, fervent torching of everybody's coats, the melting of their boots, and then the sudden, tindery conflagrations – a cereal packet left out on a kitchen surface, their books and lecture notes, the pile of magazines. The tongue became a sheet became a wall of flame.

But even when the fire had spread across the common-room floor and reached the men's door, it could not slip into their bunk room and race across the mat and their abandoned clothes to wake them in their beds. The door lips were too good a fit. Wood swells. The flames could only climb to singe and blister the outer, painted surface of their door, then set to work on the soft joists, the panels of the ceiling and the timbers of the roof.

The fire and smoke were drawn instead by their love of space towards the light and towards the open door on to the veranda where Festa slept. They sent their roasting thermals and simooms out of the furnace through the unprotected door to rape the cooler air with singed and pungent breath. If Festa woke before the flames reached her or the smoke suffocated her, she'd either have to squeeze her plump and warmly brimming self through the too-small window-panes or make her escape through the fire into the common room and out into the yard. She'd not get through the common room: within five minutes of the toppled cigarette, the overheated coffee pan, the spilt kerosene, the common room was an inferno, a box of bluing flames, containing all the gaseous wastes of burning wood. Hot walls. Hot floors. And a furnace ceiling returning its white heat on to itself until it broke through into the open air beyond the roof and sent its celebrating fireball up to the sky to glut on oxygen. Now all the self-consuming blues within the study house leaped up, five metres high, to liberate their reds and yellows on the roof.

This – the bang – was when the three men woke. Their door had lost its middle panel and the bunk room was already filling with smoke. The whole house sounded like a grounded ship, protesting timbers and collapsing joists, the fire as swelling and as rolling as the sea. It didn't take them long to spot the one way out. One of them smashed the bunk-room window with a stool then knocked out the centre struts to make a hole big enough for them to squeeze through. It didn't matter that they cut their hands and chests and didn't have time to dress or rescue any of their clothes. The flames were catching up with them and torching the two bunks and their bedding. Their oxygen had disappeared. Their lungs and legs were scorched.

It wasn't warm outside. Their naked backs were cold. Thank goodness for the flames. They stood and watched the study house blaze and carbonize. They watched the fusing and the melting of the metal pipes, the draining-board, the door handles and locks. They listened to the tom-tom of the exploding window-panes in the house and its veranda. They watched the fire attempt – and fail – to cross the remains of that once-fine garden to the outer walls and bid for freedom in the undergrowth.

It was not long before the study house was a charred and branded frame containing embers, cinders, charcoal, bone ash. All that remained (apart from a protracted claim from Festa's family against the Institute for neglect and damages) were concrete steps, foundation bricks, a sink, a seared and smelted fridge, charred and wheezing wood, the blackened metal corners of Joseph's fussy suitcase, a pall of drifting, marinating smoke and the deep, nostalgic smell of boys and bonfires.

No one could say exactly when Festa had been kippered and cremated or whether she had even had the chance to try to save her life. At first, it did not occur to the men that anyone had died. They themselves had slept too late as usual. The world would have breakfasted and gone to work before they woke. Their three missing colleagues would be where they always were by that time in the morning, down on the coast pursuing doctorates, up to their knees in flame-consuming sea.

# 15

Syl took the Friday train down to the coast, a seven-hour journey of mostly sleep and fields. It ended, late afternoon, in heavy rain, then heavy traffic during the cheap, unlicensed taxi ride to the hillside neighbourhoods in a moonlighting student's car. Her pirate fare, he said, would help to educate an architect. 'No tip for that,' she muttered to herself.

They reached the family home in fading daylight. The house, one of only three on an unmetalled side road above Deliverance Park, was dark and silent from outside, no light or radio or music. The window shutters had not been lowered but her parents' car was missing from the rattan-covered port. Syl was relieved. No car, no bodies in the house, at least. If her parents were not at home, there was still the probability they would return intact from their field trip, from their untypical delays, so that the squabbles with their daughter could begin.

Syl was nervous, nevertheless, of the empty rooms. A family home is always full of alarming corners and portentous doors, and places that are frightening to pass or face. She'd have to overcome her contempt for student architects. She asked the taxi driver – he said his name was Geo and that he was in no hurry – to come with her to check the house. And then to have a coffee or a beer, if he had the time. Who knew what she might find inside? Whatever happened, she wouldn't want to find it on her own, or have to open doors, or have to spend the evening alone without the usual comforts and distractions. Geo was convenient, as well as reasonably presentable, already mesmerized, and (she realized at once) doggedly compliant. She'd put him to good use. She might even require him to stay all night. He could prove to be a bore. His Zappa underlip, his drystone necklace and his little self-regarding name were evidence of that. But at least his car would be useful.

They parked at the bottom of the garden steps and ran up to the porch through splashing rain. Syl's hands, she was surprised to find, were trembling. She blamed it on the shaking tensions of the journey and the night of drink and dreams. She could not credit herself with any family feelings but she could hardly put the key into the lock. Geo had to do it for her. He was tense and shaking too, but for lesser reasons.

Syl took deep breaths. What had become of her? Where was the irritated, stalwart girl who only yesterday had dumped the MetroGnome in what seemed at the time like the shedding of a straitjacket? Now she felt as if her skin was too tight, that she could split and burst at any moment. This was a familiar sensation. She'd often trembled in this porch, and at this door. She'd often failed to fit the key into the lock. It was the outer chamber where, as an adolescent, she'd always had to sober up, compose her hair and clothes, rub the wildness and the chemistry from her euphoric and expanded pupils, hide her habits and her purchases, and try to reach her bed before her father, book in hand, could peer out of his room to say, 'You're late,' or ask, infuriatingly, if she had had 'an interesting evening'. To cross this threshold was to cross the Styx. Sins were discovered there, and questions asked. She would be judged. Now, no longer adolescent, in this brief shelter from the rain, the image of the Styx was doubly relevant and chilling. Something ancient and intuitive was telling her that she was entering the chambers of the dead. This was the gateway to the underworld. Geo was her ferryman. She'd have to call him Charon from now on.

The threshold of the house was swollen. The front door jammed, as ever, and Syl had to show her driver where to push to ease it open. The darkness of the house fell out into the darkness of the street. She called out cheerily from the open doorway, switching on the porch, the landing and the stairway lights, one at a time. Not panicking. They did not want to alarm anyone, particularly themselves, if anyone was there. She filled the empty spaces with her father in his dressing-gown, her mother crossing the upper landing with her hair wrapped in a towel. She even hoped to hear them say, 'You're late.'

No sound, except the drumming of the rain and those disgruntled mutterings that houses always make when lights come on.

Otherwise, everything seemed as it had always seemed, the must of books, the jackets hung across the banisters, the line of little country rugs along the wooden floor on which she'd loved to slide and ride when she was small, the pile of shoes, the pile of magazines, the bicycle her mother never used, the shadow-loving potted fern, the frame of family photographs, the clean and cooking smell of placid lives. Syl gathered up the mail from the floor and stacked it on the bottom stair. Then, holding on to Geo's jacket like a child, she started looking in the rooms. Downstairs first. The living room. The kitchen. The clutter room. The garden studio. The storage cupboard. No signs of life. Not even moths or mice. And then the upper floor.

Syl was most fearful when they reached the closed door of her mother's bedroom. Closed doors were always ominous, but when her mother's door was closed it meant, Do Not Disturb, I have a migraine, or I'm sleeping; I'm lying in the dark with Father in my arms; I'm in a temper, let me be; I am cocooned.

Syl hesitated. She even knocked, but then went in behind the taxi driver. In the few split seconds before Geo found the lamp switch and the room was snapped alive by light, she still had time to mistake the twisted shadows and misread the grey shapes on the bed.

Now, at last, there was some evidence of recent life. There was an almost empty tea-glass and a dish, the fruit rinds harvested by ants and sugar flies, on the bedside table. Her mother's cotton nightdress lay across the pillow. The bed was still unmade. One of the windows was wide open and two days of intermittent rain, dripping from the blinds, had made a wet patch on the floorboards and the rug. The bedclothes and the coverlet were damp. A book – Calvino's *Antonyms* – was on the floor. Another – *The Goatherd's Ancient Wisdom*, which she'd bought her father for his birthday, mostly to annoy him – was on the dresser under a pot of orange house spurge.

Their wedding photograph was on the wall. Syl had looked at it a thousand times before. Her parents seemed so old in it, even though they had only been in their twenties. Her age now. They were not flattered by the wedding suits or by the hard light of the flash. She stared at it as if their faces would reveal a clue. Do faces in a photograph transform on death? Were their smiles a little more fixed and thinner now, as if their mouths had reached the point beyond which there is no going on?

The studio bed in her father's room was unmade, too.

Syl checked her parents' desks and the telephone table, but they hadn't left a note of explanation for their absence. Why would they? And there was nothing on the memo pad to suggest where they had gone, no names or dates or numbers. She could not find the mobile phone, either, though she turned back all the cushions on the chairs, its usual hiding-place. They must have it with them, wherever that was. She went to see if their suitcases had been packed and taken. They had not. She opened all the mail. No clues. Just junk and bills.

Finally, while Geo made coffee for them both, Syl went outside, through the garden studio and down the slippy wooden steps. Garden rain's more welcoming and warmer than the rain in streets. She'd left every light on in the house so the deck and yard were brightly illuminated. The remains of her father's last breakfast were still on the tray next to his garden chair. His cup and saucer were filled with rain. The wooden veneer on the tray had swollen, split and lifted. Some stiffened mango peel and a mango stone were scattered on the boards. The peeling-knife had rust along its blade and tiny spiders nesting in the hollow of its clasp. All that remained of a cheese brioche was some glazed dough stuck to its wrapper. The birds had finished off the rest.

Syl was draining water off the tray when Geo called. Her coffee had been poured.

'Anything?' he asked, looking down on to the deck.

She shook her head. 'What's that? Underneath the chair.'

Her father's ledger. It was soaked, the pages corrugated by the damp, the ink reduced to winter pinks and blues. Peach blue, like chinese porcelain.

'His day book.' That was unlike her father, to let a book get wet, particularly this one.

'What was the last date he filled in?' asked Geo. The architect was brighter than he looked.

She tried to turn the pages but they tore like cotton wool. 'It's far too wet to read.'

'What will you do?'

'I'll put it in the airing room to dry.'

'No, what will you do . . . you know, to find out where they've gone?'

'I've no idea. What should I do? I'm not the police. What would you do?' She thought her tone of voice made it clear that he should not reply.

'You'll have to ask the neighbours what they know. That's first. Call up your relatives. Have you got any brothers or sisters?'

'No. I've only got an uncle left. And about a hundred second cousins. Look, let me work it out . . .'

'Phone the uncle. He might have heard from them.'

'He's in New York. I haven't seen him since I was about six. He and my father haven't talked for years. Any other inspirations?'

'Well, phone their friends.'

Syl shrugged. She couldn't put a name to any of their friends. She lived her life, not theirs.

'You'll have to check the hospitals, then. I'm sorry, but the city morgue as well. And go down to the police. Ask them to look out for the missing car. What's wrong?'

Syl made a face at him. She hated lists. She hated Things to Do. How many days of visits would that be? How much in pirate taxi fares?

'I'll need a taxi, then, for all your bright ideas,' she said.

'There's one outside.'

'I'm broke.'

'OK. I don't always have to charge. Not friends. It's Saturday tomorrow. I'm free to please myself.' He concentrated on his coffee-cup. He did not want to catch her eye, although he was content to stand out of the rain and watch the water spread across her shaved head and plaster her shirt across her breasts.

'That's good, my ferryman, my pheromone,' she said. She'd let him stay. He was the interfering sort who'd do exactly what he was told. Here, in another life, would be a fantasy come true, a chauffeur on command, a menial, a parlourman.

'How free are you to stay the night with me? I hate this house.'

They spent the night in her own bedroom – or, at least, the room that once was hers – forced together by the narrow mattress and the single sheets. Her parents had decorated since she'd left and had taken down the galaxies of luminous stars that she had stuck on the once blue ceiling. Now the Sky at Night was white and bare. The drawers and cupboards, the novel-heavy shelves of her girlhood, were empty and disinfected, like in the cheap rooms of a boarding house.

She could not sleep. Too tired and too uncomfortable. In her own apartment, she would have had some wine to help her cope with her disquiets, but her parents were not drinkers. All they had was an old and sticky bottle of honey 'rum'. No alcohol. Sober as she was, however, Syl had not needed to fake any sexual ardour with her driver. Stress and agitation, as she'd discovered on many occasions, were unexpected aphrodisiacs. So were acquiescent and dull men. She must have shocked and baffled him twenty times – and not only when she called him Charon. She brushed his penis with the stubble of her hair. She made good use of the stiff tuft below his underlip. She made his wrist and fingers ache. She made him wait. She took the opportunity to flood her parents' house with noise. But afterwards, when he was sleeping, it seemed that making love had changed and calmed her. The urgency had gone out of the search for her parents. The shadows were no longer Stygian. Death had no mystery. Anxiety had been unsexed. Now she was simply annoyed to be at home. This was a failure at her age, surely, to end up in the room were she had been a child.

In the tranquillizing darkness of the house, with sticky Geo wrapped around her back in her too narrow bed, the panic of her journey to the coast, the hasty ripping up of her own life and job, seemed idiotic and premature. She'd come more than six hundred kilometres, back to a town she hated, simply because her father's secretary had whistled. Her 'doctors', after 'a couple of days' fieldwork' – she didn't know 'exactly where' – had not turned up for work. So what? Hoorah, in fact. At last, a sign of mischief! Syl had always thought her parents loved work too much. They'd broken free for once.

Celice and Joseph had been thoughtless, possibly. But this can't have been the first time they'd gone away and not informed her or their colleagues. They'd driven somewhere in the car, a little holiday, perhaps, and overstayed. No mystery in that. There was a simple explanation for all this derangement. Her parents were too middle-aged and dull to suffer accidents or die before their time, like mountaineers or poets.

At any moment she expected to hear their old car in the street, their headlights flaring on her starless ceiling, and then the tumbling of the front-door locks as they came in and up the stairs to catch their daughter with a naked taxi driver in her bed. Here would be the slapstick answer to her father's vexing question, 'When will we get to see you in the flesh again?'

Syl was both tranquil and unnerved. She left her sleeping driver in her bed and went into her mother's room, where she would be more comfortable and might sleep. She put on her mother's nightdress and lay down on the near side of the bed where the sheets and the coverlet were dry. This would be a better welcome if they returned: they'd find their modest daughter, sleeping, and death ten thousand days away.

'To what do we owe this honour?' they'd say, sarcastic and delighted, too shy to hug. 'What brings *you* home?' Hardly anything, Syl would have to answer. That was the truth. Why had Syl come? To close the bedroom window, dry the tray and rescue Father's ledger from the rain, to make piles at the bottom of the stairs of the junk and bills from their dull and geometric lives.

# 16

Her driver woke her, shook her arm, earlier than necessary the next morning and in a bleating mood. He'd woken in the middle of the night to discover she'd abandoned him.

'Why did you go?' He was standing at the foot of Celice's bed, as peeved and naked as a child. 'I thought you'd run away.' Syl laughed. 'I've only got your word for all of this,' he said. 'Some joke.'

'That's right, I made it up. This isn't my parents' house at all. They haven't disappeared. It's just to get you into bed and save on taxi fares. You're such a catch.' She reached across and switched on the radio, the news channel, and waved the ferryman away. He'd already tried to lift the bedclothes and when she'd pulled them back in place, had gripped her wrist. 'No, there's not room in here for you. OK? Have you had breakfast yet? See what there is. Go on.'

When he had gone – he *almost* slammed the bedroom door – she listened for radio reports of local accidents and deaths. There were a few – a lorry spill, three students in a car, a garage worker crushed – but none that matched. No doctors of zoology. No unattractive people of her parents' age and learning.

Syl dressed and crept downstairs. She knew which two steps to avoid, which banister would squeak. She could see Geo kneeling in the kitchen, searching the cupboards for any edible bread. She went out in the drizzle in her father's waterproof to call on the two neighbouring houses. There was no reply at the first, except from a dog. But at the second an elderly woman she did not recognize reported, 'It's been four or five days, at least, since I've seen your mother. Or your father. Last Sunday, I think. They've not been in the yard. Their bedroom window's been hanging open. It was banging in the wind the other night. You've closed it now.' How long had her parents' car been gone? The woman didn't know. 'I wouldn't recognize their car,' she said. 'What colour is it?'

Syl wasn't sure herself. 'Have you got any bread to spare?' she asked.

Back at the house, a half-loaf richer, Syl placated Geo somewhat with a cheerful if mocking slap across his buttocks, then pulled a chair up to the phone. She tried her parents' mobile again. The number, as before, was unobtainable. She called her father's secretary. No reply, except the answerphone. The Institute was closed. Then she began to call the hospitals. The switchboards were not staffed on Saturdays. She was required to 'Key the number of the patient's ward', or 'Try again on Monday', or 'Dial four sevens for Inquiries' and join the queue of other callers and the crackling, patience-testing music of Osvaldo Bosse.

It was tempting to get rid of Geo straight away. Already he was getting on her nerves. He was a whiner and a liability. She did not like the way he'd held her arm once he'd sniffed her out in Mother's bed that morning. Nor his attempts to lift the coverlet and join her there. Then, once she had scrumped the half-loaf, he evidently thought she was obliged to get him breakfast. 'I've given up waitressing,' she'd said, and let him sulk. But now she guessed she'd better change her tune, at least till evening. If, as seemed likely, she couldn't get through to the hospitals by phone, then a driver and his car would be essential for the day.

Then she'd dump him. ('You'll have to find yourself another girl. Your lovemaking is poisonous. Geo's such a very stupid name. Don't phone.')

He was no longer in the kitchen when Syl went to make her peace. She found him in the garden studio, sitting in her father's chair with coffee, an apple and an old newspaper. He'd rather die than have to toast himself some bread. He, surely, was the guest, the giver of free lifts, who should be fussed by her.

'Sorry, Ferryman,' she said.

'OK.'

'I'm worried, see?' She put her arms around his shoulders. 'Shall we go?'

'Go where?'

'Go to the hospitals, I guess. And then go to the dungeons where the ghouls and corpses are. Frequent the graveyards and the tombs. Hang out at funerals.' She did her best to cheer him up. She put her hand inside his shirt.

'OK,' he said, as flatly as he could.

But first Syl went upstairs to shower and then to make her mother's bed. She had to clear away the breakfast-cup and plate, and remove her parents' ghostly residues. She took the rain-soaked rug and coverlet from her mother's bedroom and hung them in the airing room. Her father's ledger was already dry and stiff. She was reluctant to look inside. This was his private space, and no child wants to read about a father's secret world. Nevertheless, she held up the pages to the window light and let them hang open until she found the last completed page. The paper had expanded and the ink had lost its pigment, first to the rain, now to the heat. The ledger smelt of museums and the inside of briefcases. But still his final, corrugated sentence was clear enough. Such joyful, optimistic words, she thought. And reassuring. He'd written, 'Tuesday. Far too fine for work.' And then, '(In search of sprayhoppers!)'.

So Syl, with Geo too attentive and long-suffering at her side, embarked upon the oddest town tour that Saturday, driving in the wake of Fish through rain-dejected streets, with only one windscreen wiper functioning on his car, from clinic to hospital, the private and the public wings, hoping to find Joseph and Celice tucked up in bed with grapes and magazines. They ran up stairs, rode bed-wide lifts, and queued for clerks to hunt her parents' names on screens and registers. They visited the wards of unclaimed, injured patients who might be Joseph or Celice, pulling back the curtains to see the damage that a car, a knife, a heart-attack or an overdose can do. All strangers.

Finally, they visited the central police station. Syl did her best to alarm the duty officer with how reliable and punctual her parents usually were. 'They're the ones who always let you down,' he said. He took descriptions of her parents and noted the registration number of their car. He searched his VDU, but no reports were listed.

'They'll show up,' he promised. And then, an agile contradiction, 'Check they haven't turned up at the city morgue.'

# 17

Birdie volunteered to run down to the beach to check that Festa, Joseph and Celice were indeed safe and to let them know about the fire and what was lost inside the study house; their clothes and bags, their notes and books, the promise of their doctorates. Birdie could hardly refuse the task: he was the fittest of the three and, actually, the only one with any shoes. He'd used the heels to knock the glass out of the bunk-room windows for their escape.

Hanny and Victor would have to make their unheroic ways barefoot across the manac fields towards the shanty village. A second visit, less triumphant than the first, in search of borrowed clothes and shoes, and a telephone to call the Institute, the airport and the fire brigade. If this wind picked up, so might the embers of the study house. Then they'd have a forest or a scrub fire to account for, and even houses in the village might be lost. A trembling thought.

Their comrade Birdie was a scarecrow, leaping down the steps, two at a time, through the stands of flute bushes, until he reached the farm lane and the ponds. He wore only a white T-shirt, fly-fronted pyjama bottoms from which his penis pecked and nodded like a finger puppet as he ran, black ankle boots, no socks. He smelt of smoke and sweat. His hair was matted. He'd never felt before so cinematic and so wholly ludicrous. He knew where on the coast he would find his three colleagues. He had himself helped Festa rake in the seaweed for her medical and nutritional studies one afternoon. She'd recompensed him with her kisses just the night before, although, despite his best endeavours, she was not yet quite ready to allow his tongue to penetrate her lips or his hand to dip into her clothes. And he had twice spotted Joseph and Celice in the shallows further up the coast, towards the jutting foreshore of the bay.

The route was simple and mostly downhill: the pines, the marshes and the dunes, the coastal track, the wide expanses of the beach, the splashing run along the shore towards the figures in the tide, the distant, bending plume of ash. He hadn't felt so fit for months, despite the ankle-rubbing boots and the remains of a smoke-laden headache. He was pumped up by all the thrilling chemicals of shock. The effort brought it home to him. Death had been near; he had been fortunate. He'd never been so fast or spirited, so oddly close to nausea and joy. How glorious he would appear to Festa as he called to her, half naked and half Hollywood, an envoy bearing messages and running from the fire towards the sea.

# 18

It would have been a busy week for death even without Syl's parents. One hundred and twenty-seven new bodies had been registered at the city morgue before the clerk went off for lunch. And Fish would send a further seventeen in the afternoon when the clerk came back to work, puffed up as usual at that time on a Saturday by barbiturates. He'd already reached the fourth level of disinhibition and euphoria by swallowing two Eden pills with his lunch-time beer. Now he was chewing Go gum to take away the smell of onions, cigarettes and alcohol. Cadavers and lunch do not mix well, he had been told a hundred times by the duty doctor. A morgue worker should be as sweet-breathed as a dentist or a prostitute. A belching clerk should not deal with the deceased and their bereaved. Whispered sympathies to widows and to widowers – and to daughters who had lost both parents in a single day – could not come laden with the stench of food and nicotine and still appear sincere.

But the clerk was not, yet, the sort to seem sincere even when his breath was sweet. He resented working in the morgue. It showed. He hated having to dispense his sympathy to strangers. Like most young men, he had no time for death or grief. The bodies had no poetry. He was too sharp and fun-loving, he thought, to waste his life on them. The duty doctors were a bunch of fools to think that lunch and cadavers do not mix well and that a belching clerk should not deal with the deceased and their bereaved. You'd think the duty doctors had never touched a cadaver. The dead don't talk – but bodies belch for hours after death. A woman bends to kiss her husband for the final time. Despite the warnings of the morgue attendant – sweet-breathed or not – she puts a little weight upon his chest, and is rewarded with the stench of every meal she's cooked for him in forty years. The morgue could sound, at times, as if a ghoulish choir was warming up, backed by a wind ensemble of tubas and bassoons. It could smell as scalpy, scorched and pungent as a hairdressing salon. The breath of these cold choristers was far worse than the onion breath of clerks. But no one said that bodies weren't sincere. There's nothing more sincere than death. The dead mean what they say.

The morgue clerk ran his finger down the register, as usual, not fearful of what he might encounter but half expecting and half hoping to find a name he recognized. Fish might oblige him with a neighbour, say, or some young man who'd been a good friend at his school, or one of his many neglected aunts. Anything to break the tedium of work. He'd find his own name on the list one day, one of the duty doctors had warned him. *Enfin*, a name to make his heart stand still. Sincere, at last.

It was the clerk's job to record the deceased's name on its last form, the place of birth, the date of death, the cause, a doctor's signature, the registrar's smudged stamp, a job number, a label, and then to check the disposition of the bodies on his charts so that he could allocate a storage space. It was full house, that weekend matinée, when Syl came looking for her parents, preceding them in fact. The refrigerated drawers, other than the ones that were being cleaned or serviced by the techs, were all occupied. Some would become empty again after two o'clock when relatives could claim their deceased and buy the regulation cardboard casket in which to bear the body home.

Syl and Geo were the first inquirers after lunch. The woman's parents had gone missing, she explained, the usual dreadful trepidation on her face. They'd like to check amongst the dead, if that was possible. 'Sent by the police,' the man added, as if such information made a difference. The clerk ran his fingers down the list of dead again. No Joseph or Celice. Were any of the bodies in the morgue unidentified?

'Plenty,' said the clerk. 'You want to look? Wait there.' He popped another Go gum in his mouth and offered one to Syl. Not to the man 'sent by the police'. He was attracted to the woman's new-mown hair and her unruly face. A potent combination. The libertine, the nun. Here was a face that knew no bounds. He'd find the time and opportunity to go with her up to the fridge. Without the man, of course.

Syl and Geo sat and waited, without speaking, for more than half an hour until a woman in her sixties, with her two sons, arrived. She rang the handbell on the ledge outside the clerk's room. 'My sister died,' she said, when he pulled back the glass. 'They took her for an autopsy.'

He checked the number on her form against his charts. 'She's here. Upstairs.'

'Where can we bring the van?'

The clerk told the brothers how to find the basement entry to the morgue, then called the woman and Syl to follow him.

'Sorry, you have to be a blood relative,' he lied to Geo. 'She won't be long.' He led the women up the stairs, not speaking, to the storage rooms. He found the sister's name again on the inventory but no one had written down the drawer number. 'You'll recognize her, will you? If we look . . .'

'She is my sister . . .'

'No problem, then. So long as you're sure. Mistakes are made.' He turned to Syl, and winked, complicitly. The young against the old. 'And you can see if there's anyone you recognize. OK?'

The clerk – Fish's rakish protégé, its representative on earth – was in the best of moods, despite the work. Barbiturates and beer. He quite enjoyed his visits to the fridge. It was always interesting and often amusing to accompany a person deputized to identify a corpse. No easy task. Often distant cousins or short-sighted neighbours were sent rather than expose a wife or daughter to the trauma. A cousin or a neighbour can be a virtual stranger. You might pass one in the street and not be recognized. And so indeed, as the morgue clerk had warned, mistakes were made, the dead were sometimes misidentified. Death is a deep disguise. The eyelids of the body might be taped, perhaps, or the mouth tied shut with a crêpe scarf round the head. Or someone could have made the error, after the stroke or heart-attack had done its job, of taking out the fellow's dentures. Rigor mortis had set in and now the man's mouth had changed shape. The one-and-all-time fat man had become a hermit monk, thinned by prayers and fasting, hollow-cheeked. His facial muscles had collapsed. The teeth would not fit back. The morgue technician had either put the dentures in a plastic bag tied to the body's thumb or simply hooked them round the dead man's gums, covering the lips. A flesh and plastic tribute to Picasso for the cousin or the neighbour to identify.

Or else the corpse's face, not helped by wads of cotton wool, was bloated. A man who'd been cadaverous for sixty years was now, in death, as full and smooth as a pumpkin mask.

Or else a bored technician might have shaved away a distinguishing moustache, just for the fun of it, or disguised a birthmark with his panstick.

For those deputed relatives and friends, the body's face was never quite the one that they had known or loved. The displayed person could be anyone, in fact. We share expressions when we're dead. All cousins look the same. So, yes, they'd try to recognize the corpse through their slit eyes as quickly as they could. They'd nod. They'd turn away. A tiny glimpse should be enough. They'd sign the forms provided by the clerk and, once in a while, take the wrong body from the morgue disguised and hidden by the cardboard coffin, almost convinced by what they'd seen.

'I've known of people that've been buried by complete strangers,' the clerk was always pleased to tell his friends. He had a hundred Gothic anecdotes of misplaced cadavers and comic funerals. Shocking and hilarious, but not for public airing. He had to save his embellished and unlikely stories for the bar: the one occasion, for example, when mourners at a spinster's funeral had found an old man dead in the casket instead of the expected woman scarcely forty years of age; the time, ten years before, when a technician's resourceful use of a condom and some orange garden string had gone expensively wrong – the relatives had sued the morgue; the story of the body that had snored for seven nights.

So the clerk was hoping to be amused when he took the two women to the robing room. He concentrated on Syl's back and hair as she removed her jacket and put on the knee-length polymura coat he'd issued. Less than flattering, usually. But irresistible on her. Then he let them into the antechamber of the morgue. A thirty-metre fridge. A line of double sinks, with elbow taps and shelves of fluids, powders and cosmetics. A line of haz-mat bins. A metal tank. A row of hooks and hangers. A washing-line with dripping sheets. Beyond, through rubber doors, the cheerful music from a radio, and voices.

'This way,' he said, backing into the doors and touching both women lightly on their polymura'd elbows as they passed through. 'Don't mind the smell.'

The smell, in fact, was tolerable – not death, but industry – some solvents, disinfectants and detergents and the tinny odour of wet floors. The five men working here were clones in surgical gowns, green gloves, thick rubber aprons, their faces hidden by white masks and splatter glasses. Each had a body on a marble table with metal guttering. Preparing them for burial. For one, a gentle massage of the arms to break down rigor mortis. A second body dipped and whitened to the soft attentions of a disinfectant swab. Another had small puncture holes, and its attendant was poking in a trocar tube for drawing off the fluids from its cavities. The fourth was being beautified: his wounds and half-formed scabs were masked by theatrical cosmetics, panstick and rouge. It wasn't right to bury him if he was looking dead. The last body was being silenced for eternity; the morgue's best seamster drew needle and thread through the jaw and nostril to close the dead man's mouth.

'Try not to look,' the clerk said, sweeping ahead into Left Luggage, a room packed floor to roof with metal lockers. 'Now take your time.'

Starting with the bank of drawers behind the door, he began to slide the corpses into view, feet first, like mannequins. Most of the bodies had labels tied round their toes with their names, the date, time and cause of death printed on them. But some were anonymous, and then the clerk had to pull back the paper shroud to show the face. 'Just shake your head,' he said. 'Is this one yours?' He knew that people were not used, as he was, to the smell. They would not want to speak and taste the air.

How could anybody, except a writer of bad songs, think that death was sweet, soft as a petal when it came, and 'bathed in perfumes of sad joy'? The only perfumes that the techs employed were disinfectants or the mix of lime and alcohol with which they swabbed the bodies to remove the mess and to close the pores. No lime or alcohol was strong enough to make them sweet and soft. The orifices and the vents, the bodies' doors and windows, had not been closed by death. The smell was sweat and pickles, bacon rind and eggs, toilets, rubber, cordite and volcanoes.

As Syl and her companion were discovering, bodies defecate and piss while they are dying. They continue to smell badly till there's nothing left but bone. Relatives should not – as many do – remove the cotton from the rectum or the vagina when they've reclaimed their body for its lying in, the clerk explained with the tones of a helpful shop assistant detailing fabric care. That would be to take the stopper from the drain. Nor should they touch whatever they discover in the penis. It has been put there for a good purpose, not a joke. The clerk would not pull back a sheet to show them what he meant but they could imagine, he was sure. The penis is a comedy when it is dead and best kept hidden. 'Not erections, funnily,' he said, made reckless and loquacious by Syl's wild face and by the Eden pills dissolving in his blood. 'But . . .' a lowered voice, to demonstrate discretion '. . . the waste.' He had sense enough to bite his tongue and say no more. The women could not be so easily amused as his male friends – though it was a tempting prospect just to show them one of the morgue's little plastic stoppers. 'Made for the purpose,' he could say. 'Reusable. Fits all sizes.' That'd cause a stir.

The women, though, did not even notice that the clerk was smiling to himself. They were too overawed by the clank and contents of the body-heavy drawers, by all the different ways and shapes of death. This was not the town nor was it the season for plagues or viruses. The weather was too salty. But as the clerk's two visitors browsed – in silence now – amongst the men and women in the morgue that Saturday afternoon and read the labels wrapped around the ankles of the cadavers, they should have found a pattern to the deaths. The heart-attack was suspect number one. Early morning was the favour-ite time of death. Then midnight and pneumonia. Next suspect killer was the motor-car. And then the cancers, mostly caused by drink or cigarettes or by the sea-swarf in the wind-borne salt. Stop breathing if you do not want to die. Don't drive, don't smoke, don't cross a road, don't drink, don't go to restaurants, don't eat the region's heavy specialities, the crab and suet casserole, the lardy nut quadroon, the egg liqueur, the blue-cheese sauce.

At last – the sixty-seventh drawer – they found the woman's sister. There was no label on her toe. But she was certain who it was, though shocked to see how wasted she appeared: 'I'd been speaking to her just before she went. She sounded absolutely fine.'

The clerk came forward and put his arms around the women's backs. Their opportunist comforter. He hardly touched the sister's sobbing shoulders, but he spread his hand quite heavily across Syl's waist. His lifted thumb could feel her body and her shirt through the thin polymura.

'It's not an easy time,' he said. His little finger pressed her back.

'Have we checked everything?' Syl said. She shook his hand away.

'Not quite.' He led them to the coroner's examination room where there were twelve more refrigerated drawers. These were the murders – only one 'in stock' that day – and, of course, the suicides that had outwitted Fish's damp embraces. Eleven suicides. More than was proper for a town this size. There'd been an epidemic of self-loathing. Better to kill than to die. There was a woman rattling with pills. Two gassings. A poisoning. A short attempt at flight from the roof of an office building. A student hanging on her rope. This one had made a tape-recorded message regretting all the trouble she had caused. She'd left the cassette, now with the coroner, on a table top, level with her swinging knees. In the drawer below her – once, briefly, the penultimate resting place of the

Academic Mentor – was a policeman who'd been caught shoplifting. A pair of trousers. Hardly worth the risk. He knew he'd be dismissed, no doubt of that. Imprisoned, even, as an example to any of his colleagues who might be similarly tempted. He'd lose his pension with his job. So he'd climbed the steps to the naval monument in his green parade uniform and finished himself with a shotgun, a bullet through his cap and head. The rumour was that someone long wanted by the police had been arrested for the death.

There were the bodies of two euthanasists, as well. And what remained of a young man and his wife who had set light to their small room.

The clerk pulled open the last remaining drawer for Syl. This was the murderee, a rich young man with narrow lips and the tussock hairstyle that had been fashionable five years before. She shook her head. Nobody had resembled either of her parents.

'Then they're not dead,' he said. 'If they were dead they'd have a drawer by now. Come on.' He took them to the discharge room and called into the Tannoy for someone to bring a gurney and a cardboard casket for the sister's body. He filled in a release form and, when the body was brought in, accompanied the women and the corpse into the service elevator. He let the sister speak. They always wanted to speak as soon as he pulled back the railing doors to make the draughty, ponderous descent to the loading bay. He only had to smile and nod. He didn't have to listen.

'She was my only sister,' the woman said to them both, but mostly fixing Syl with her wet eyes. 'She'd only taken a toothbrush from its cup. It must have weighed like lead. Tore the muscles in her arm and chest.' They'd heard her cry in pain, she explained. It took her down. She'd hit her chin on the sink, and almost bit her tongue in half. Her niece saw her body, on the floor, then her bloody mouth. The niece had been a nurse, so guessed the aunt had had a brain haemorrhage. She did not try to activate her lungs or heart. It was too late, anyway. They couldn't even prise the toothbrush from her grip. There was the blood. Then the dreadful smell of Fish. And everybody realized that she was gone for good. 'To think, she never had a day off sick in all her life. And then, fuff, fuff, she's . . . you know, done for.'

Syl held the woman's arm, to steady her for the descent. The clerk kept well away until they reached the basement. Then he took charge of the gurney again, and helped to lift and slide the casket into the brothers' hired van. They slipped him money, for his help. 'Good luck,' he said, and muttered, 'Give her a decent send-off.' The woman and her sons were almost smiling when they drove away. Everybody was relieved to have the body in the house the night before the burial, lying in its own bed in its own home, amongst its things.

'What should we do?' asked Syl.

The clerk, standing at the elevator gate, just shrugged. He'd like to have her warm and naked on a slab, his scissors slicing through her polymura coat. 'We've looked,' he said. 'There's nowhere else. Go to the police. Check up at all the hospitals.'

'We've done all that.'

He closed the gate and pointed through the concertina'd bars up the ramp to the street. 'That way.' And then – you could never know your luck with a woman like her – he added, 'Do call again!'

By the time that Syl was half-way up the ramp the clerk had already found the little bag of Eden pills. He popped a couple underneath his tongue. They were as easily absorbed as sugar. So once he'd reached the morgue to log out the woman's body from his register, the new pills had begun to have their topping up effect. Nothing mattered any more. His little pills could conquer all the stench and tedium of death. They shrank the afternoon.

'She'll not be long,' he said to Geo. The idiot was still sitting on the waiting bench, as chained and patient as a dog. You'd see more vigour in the fridge, the morgue clerk thought, and spent a mean and happy half-hour before the couple finally found each other and departed from his life if not his fantasies.

That night, Syl conquered death by sleeping with her driver once again. It had been a wearing day. She could not spend the evening alone. She'd rather tolerate his proprietorial love-making for a second time, his too-long fingernails, his inexperience, his lack of enterprise. It was a necessary sacrifice, and soon dispatched.

This time – an awful and pre-emptive sin – they took her mother's bed. Dry sheets. More space. But as she prepared to let her ferryman help himself to her, the phone rang in the hall. Her chest went tight. She had to gasp for breath – what had become of her disdain for family? – and run out on to the landing. She could only stutter nonsense when she picked up the receiver, trembling and naked in the moonlit house. Good news or bad? Please let there be a parent on the phone. It was the police, of course. They'd found the car, downtown, abandoned in a bank car park. A thief had taken out the radio-cassette, but otherwise no damage. No sign of any accident or forced entry. No keys. There was a receipt for parking on the dashboard, timed and dated Tuesday noon, for the open ground next to the visitors' centre beyond the airport road out at Baritone Bay. 'Is there any reason you can think of why your parents would go there?'

# 19

**Noon**

It was not the easy and pleasant walk that he had promised
her. There was a level, waymarked track down to the coast,
but Joseph and Celice had to clamber through the man-made
hillocks on the margins of the widened airport road and
skirt the recent piles of building aggregate to reach the high
backshores where once the study house had been. Instead of
beaten scrub, the soil was loose and gravelly. The rubble-loving
undergrowth tore at their trouser legs. Somewhere, below
these engineering dunes, Celice had first seen Joseph, almost
thirty years before. He'd slipped and pulled the muscles in his
back. The other men – it *didn't* seem like yesterday – had had
to help him with his antique, boned suitcase. Consumed by
fire. The well-worn path that the six students had followed
then had disappeared over time, of course. There was no
longer any need for it. No study house, no path.

Celice was breathless, not only from the effort of the climbs
on such a sun-wrecked day but also with apprehension. The
blackened wreckage of her past was far too close – six hundred
metres from the air-conditioned comforts of their car. She'd
never found the time or felt the impulse to return before. Not
cowardice, just caution. Why take the risk? Why resurrect bad
memories? It isn't true that murderers are drawn back to the

scene of crime before the blood has dried. They only dare go back when age has toughened them.

Celice was not a fool. She knew her thirty-year timidity had not been rational. Yet the fire had singed and carbonized her past. She was in no doubt of that. She could hardly bear even to recollect her first meeting with her husband, his singing voice, the sprayhoppers, their first love-making, because an image of the smoking study house would soon impose itself. With Festa's blackened face, her toasted hair. And Festa's melted voice.

Celice hadn't witnessed a single flame of the actual fire, of course. She'd been . . . elsewhere. Impossibly alive and joyful. By the time that she and Joseph had finished with each other at Baritone Bay, the fire had used up all the wood and was only ruminating smoke. The almost naked ornithologist, running in black boots and his nightwear along the coastal track, had found them – caught them – consummated, arm in arm, coming from the dunes. 'Thank God,' he'd said, and almost hugged them with relief. 'Where's Festa?'

Celice could still recall her easy shrug. She hadn't cared where Festa was. But some days, now and ever since, that's all she thought about. Where Festa was. Her thirty years of being dead. The life in parallel to hers that Celice's colleague never led. The uncompleted doctorate. The unbegun career. The unique progress never made in the medical and nutritional uses of seaweed. The man not found, the children she'd not have, the house, the undemanding life. The middle years of that enraging voice and spongy laugh. The thinning of the thick, loose hair. The fattening. The chance encounters with Celice, once in a while, on the street or at the annual conference on seaweed studies, 'It's Festa, isn't it? . . . How's life with you? I haven't seen you since . . .' All murdered by a coffee pan or by a toppling cigarette.

It was a flinty task for Celice even to imagine herself back at the study house, as she'd last seen it, standing, trembling, with another calming cigarette and facing down across the black and silvered ruin towards a smoke-smudged sea. Her lungs, already stressed by their uphill running from the coast, had been raw with wood ash. She'd yelled out Festa's name, both at the house and at the countryside around, until her voice had failed. But no one answered her – and no one ever would. Her colleague and room-mate was buried underneath the smouldering tent of timbers. It was too hot to peer more closely and look for signs of skull and bones or rake the ash for Festa's confirmation ring, her watch, her silver bracelet and her teeth.

Joseph had come forward to put his arm around her waist. But she had waved him back. It was his fault, this fire, this death, as well as hers. Love was to blame, and passion. Passion such as theirs, brief as it was, was strong enough to shake the balance of the natural world, and test its synchronicity. Where there is sex, then there is death. They are the dark co-ordinates of one straight line. Grief is death eroticized. And sex is only shuffling off this mortal coil before its time to plummet to the post-coital afterlife. Celice's haste to rush out of the house and take command of her new love so early in the morning was bound to set the flame. That is a scientific view.

Who ought to take responsibility at times like this? There always has to be a volunteer. When the airport hydrant, two firemen and a policeman had arrived to dampen the embers and begin the search for Festa's remains, the two men there – Celice's lover and the ornithologist – said they could not suggest or even guess how the fire had started. It was a mystery. They had no theories so they could accept no guilt. But Celice, not noticeably self-sacrificing in lesser matters, was eager for the blame. Embraced it, actually. She knew her only shelter was the truth. She half remembered seeing the kerosene lamp under the table, she admitted to the policeman. She couldn't say whether or not it was still alight when she'd got up and hurried out that morning.

'Let's get this right. You left a lamp to burn all night? Underneath a wooden table?' The policeman's prejudices were reconfirmed. Here was a science graduate with a fine accent and no expenses spared who hadn't yet found out that wood was combustible and that flames were hot. 'That takes the prize,' he said. But there was more. Celice could not stop confessing, despite Joseph's restraining touch in the small of her back. That was a touch she hated all her life. She would not hide behind white lies or plead ignorance like him. She told the policeman, then, about the boiling coffee pan and her smouldering, toppling cigarettes. She'd later write to Festa's parents, repeating all her burning truths. She'd admit the same again in court for the inquiry judge.

Now, middle-aged and only half as reckless as she'd once been, Celice was hiding in her husband's wake as he pushed through the undergrowth of untrimmed shrubs to the side of the study house's tumbled western wall. Joseph had been behind her as they'd crossed the rubble hills. But he had taken too many opportunities to help her on the loose earth and the gradients by spreading his fingers flat across her bottom and pushing. This was a lover pushing her, looking for the acqui-escent flesh, and not a simple helping hand. She was annoyed. What had come over him? Could he not guess how tense she was? Or how angry she remained at his dishonest and restraining touch that age ago?

Sometimes she feared that there was nothing grand in their relationship, nothing to secure her loyalty or admiration, even, since that first encounter with his singing voice, that great sustaining wave on which her love had surfed for almost thirty years. Where had been the zest since then? Where, indeed, had been their common ground? She had become the pepper to his salt. They were the fruit of different, and opposing, trees.

So many times she'd asked herself, Why had their love proved troublesome? Celice could count the ways. First, she was a warrior by nature, unafraid of battle, quick to raise her fists. Her husband was an appeaser, loath even to raise his voice. She was assaulted and defeated, when they argued, by his lazy patience and his infuriating tact. After any argument she was mostly angry for one week. And he was eloquently hurt for two. Second, as she grew older, she wanted company and friends; he was unsociable and courted privacy. Next, she was dissatisfied with her life; he was only anxious about his. She wanted everything to get better; he was nervous that all the hard-earned certainties might disappear – he'd lose his health, his work, his monkish peace of mind. She had no fear of death. He cowered from it all the time, and lived his middle years with one foot on the bottom rung of a descending ladder, ready for the looming fall, the streak of blood in his urine, the tell-tale black deposits on the toilet paper, the colonizing lumps and swellings that he seemed to search for twenty times a day, the sharp pains in the arms and chest, the sudden stroke. He had become obsessed with symmetry: two legs aching was old age; one leg aching was a clot, arthritis or a growth. Lastly, he saw their marriage as a success; she was unsatisfied by it. Despite their early promise and ambitions they had not left as many marks upon the world as she had hoped. One daughter was the only product of their lives – and one that was not promising, pretended to no plans, and had fled from the family home as if it were a prison cell. Celice's audit of herself and her long years with Joseph was not uplifting. Their legacy, she'd be the first to say, would be less than their inheritance.

Yet there still was love, the placid love that only time can cultivate, a love preserved by habit and by memory. Their tree had little rising sap, perhaps, but it was held firm by deep and ancient roots. Old, lasting love. Celice had never doubted it. Their marriage had initiating strengths. A great sustaining wave, no matter how old, is more than most couples can boast of and enjoy. Her husband angered her, perhaps, from time to time. Most of the time, in fact. He was too weak and watery. And she was disappointed with herself. But their beginnings were indelible and strong. Joseph could still evoke for her – infrequently – those sentimental choruses, that great subversive bass, that guiding star, that midnight bride, the peaking of her body and the song in that far, haunted place. When they were young.

Yet this was not a haunted place, as it turned out. The study house was fertile ground for rock shrubs and carbon-loving plants. The bunk room and the common room were oblong beds of stoveweed and pyrosia, the green bells of the one almost a perfect match for the high bracts of the other. The last remains of bricks, masonry and walls were colonized by nettles, brambles, buddleia and mortar roses. The house was razed but the architect's blue building plans were still adhered to by the plants. What roof beams had survived the fire and years, were skeletal, stripped of all the charring, tapered by erosion, and clad in the reds and greens of timber algae.

Celice stepped across the porch stone and walked into the middle of the common room, next to the almost buried sink. The doorway to the veranda was now two heaps of weed. There was no evidence of any building on that side of the house. The scrubby backshore plants, the hollow-stemmed flute bushes and the thorns had colonized the long rectangle of the glass veranda and were growing deeply. Celice could not reach the spot where she and Festa had spread their mattresses and sleeping-bags, and shared their cigarettes. She squatted on her heels and peered beneath the bushes. What did she expect? Some bones? A snake? A woman, sitting up in bed? The red glow of tobacco? The odours of a barbecue? A scream? The sudden ending of her guilt as if the study house had pardons to give out?

The smell was only vegetation and the sound was only leaves and stalks. All she found to show that there had once been shelter here were shards of grey and thinning glass, a riddled piece of corrugated iron, and what could be the rusting helix of a mattress spring. She was tempted to say something to Festa, but did not. She might have, if she'd been by herself. An apology, perhaps. A reassurance of some kind. But Joseph was in hearing range. He wouldn't understand. Men had no emotional imagination, she had found. That's why he hadn't felt the guilt she'd felt. That's why the death of Festa had been so readily survived by him. Perhaps, that's why men were more stable than the women she knew. They accepted the eerie truth of life and death, that one is passing and the other is conclusive. We live, we die, we do not need to understand. There are no ghosts to lay. There is just ash and memory.

Celice was still shaking and a little nauseous when she walked back through the denuded common room to join her husband for the walk down to the coast. She took deep breaths. The anticlimax had been shocking. How little she had felt. How tearless she had been. How mute the ruins were.

'Not what I expected,' she said. 'So much has grown here. I thought it would be bleak.' She should have known – a doctor of zoology – that vegetation would have buried all the past, that death would be absorbed.

Mondazy wrote, 'Our Books of Life don't have an end. Fresh chapters are produced though we are dead. Our pages never terminate. But, given time, the paper yellows, then turns green. The vellum flesh becomes the leaf.'

# 20

Syl would not speak to her conscripted driver as they drove through the slums and hinterlands of their drenched coastal town that Sunday afternoon. No one about. It seemed, at times, as if they were travelling through still photographs. Life as it always was, fixed in its frame, just there at just that time. No one had died, or ever could.

Syl was in a spiteful mood and sitting in the back. Her lover ought to know exactly what his status was. He was too vain and immature to comprehend that his raw caresses in her mother's bed, his constant touching of her arm, his sudden, uninvited kisses were not a welcome comfort. They were his taxi fares. She drummed her fingers on her knees. But Geo was already accustomed to her early-morning tempers and her surprising appetites at night. He'd never known such cruelty and boldness or guessed how stimulating they could be. He watched her through the rear-view mirror: she sat with her legs drawn up and her head against the side window of his car, looking at the empty streets, the timber yards, the shuttered bars, the occasional clinker lorry going to and from the Salt Pines building sites. He knew she was defying him to make a sound. Thank goodness Geo was a willing soul, and so naïve. He thought he understood her need for silence and her constant irritation. Anxiety, of course. Grief and fear. And the irresistible drama of the spotlight. He could not blame himself for her fixed mouth and her turned head.

They parked at the visitors' centre, where Joseph and Celice had parked, five days before, and from where their car had almost certainly been stolen. The lot was almost full. The building had been taken over by the police as its headquarters. There were squad jeeps, a catering trailer, a radio van with its aerial raised, and the unmarked cars of the detectives lined up across the gravel. Four Sunday anglers in an open jeep were being turned away by the uniformed auxiliaries guarding the entrance to the centre. The coast was closed. Except to planes. The police were powerless to close the skies. Two Dorkers and a noisy One-One-Eight, piloted by weekend hobby fliers, were stunting in the thermals off the bar.

Syl, it's true, *was* indulging herself. After the stifling dol-drums of the drive with Geo it was a sudden and an unexpected stimulant to be the centre of so much respectful attention. She'd only had to tell one of the guards, 'I'm the daughter,' for the makeshift barrier to be lifted and for their car to be conducted in as if its occupants were honoured guests, dignified by their proximity to death. She liked the way that no one tried to stare at her. They looked down at their shoes as she walked by. She was the Empress of Japan, foremost and unapproachable. To catch her eye with theirs would be a violation.

This was unusual for Syl – the deference of uniforms. Usually her dress, her age, the way she spoke, her hard-cropped hair would trigger animosity from the police, and a bag search. Now, for once, she could savour their sombre bustle, their measured urgency, their lowered eyes and voices. She could enjoy herself. That's the blushing ambiguity of deaths and, particularly, of dramatic deaths like this. The closest family, the principal mourners are oddly happy with themselves, and stirred. Their hearts – and social niceties – may call for frenzies of despair, an ululating epilepsy, collapse, hysteria, but their brains dispense instead a cocktail of euphoric chemicals to bolster them against the shock and rage. Adrenalin cannot discriminate. The stimulant and tranquillizer pumps usurp the promptings of the heart. They make death seem invigorating, and erotic. Syl felt – bizarrely – closer to laughter than to tears. She was excited, almost glad, to be the daughter of the dead, to be so irritated, and so estranged from Joseph and Celice, to be so mean and careless with the ferryman, yet seem so dutiful, capable and strong to all the uniforms. The awful truth had not sunk in. The deaths were still not real. She only fell apart once she'd descended fifty metres of the track and saw the world's most mournful sight, the wide expanse of wind-whipped beach and sea, the inter-tide.

It was just as well that Geo wasn't there to put his arm around Syl and make things worse. He hadn't taken much persuading not to walk with her along the coast to inspect the bodies. He was a little squeamish. She'd rather be alone, she said. He understood. He would have kissed her there and then, as she escaped the car. To do so would establish his 'lover' status in the eyes of the police. How jealous they would be if they could know how that cropped head had burrowed into him. Besides, he would not wish to be mistaken for a cousin or a neighbour, or spot-fined for operating an unlicensed cab. He'd pursed his lips and tipped his head towards her. But she had pressed her fingers on his chest to keep his face away. Syl was relieved to leave him in the car park, a bruised look on his face, like a disappointed spaniel denied its exercise. She'd go alone, the orphan on the coast. But one of the officers inside the centre had instructed a policewoman to accompany her. Now with the first sight of the sea and her first tears Syl wanted privacy even more. Emotion was embarrassing. She told her escort that she was not needed. The woman, probably no older than Syl herself, just nodded. 'But we have a policy,' she said, 'at any scene of crime.'

'I have a policy, as well.' Quite what it was, Syl didn't know, unless it was always to argue with a uniform.

So they agreed a compromise. The policewoman would follow twenty metres behind, a stalking guard, an aide, but not a companion. Syl could be the Empress of Japan again, embarking on her solitary wake.

The call to the coast had come at midday while Syl was sitting on the deck at home, in her father's chair, still in her mother's dressing-gown and waiting for her hired hand to bring some cake and coffee. She'd heard the phone: 'You answer it,' she shouted. Geo wrote the message down like some dull waiter and brought it out to her. Two bodies had been found by police dogs in the salt dunes at Baritone Bay. Near where they must have parked the car. Could she come out at once? Identify her mother and her father?

How would Syl cope?

At first she coped by pouring all her scorn on Geo. 'Was that all?' she asked. Hadn't the police said anything about the cause of death? He shook his head. A lifelong dope. 'You didn't think to ask, of course. A mere detail.'

He didn't need to ask, in fact. Syl knew. She'd always known. That was why her first glimpse of the sea that afternoon had summoned those first tears. This was her parents' programmed death. They'd drowned at last. That was the only likely way that Celice and Joseph would die before their times. They drove too carefully to crash their car, except in dreams. Her mother had weaned herself off cigarettes. They hardly drank. They touched their toes ten times a day. They ate like scientists, a perfect balance between their carbohydrates and their nutrients, their vitamins and oils. They'd not take any risks. They did not walk down unlit streets with glinting jewellery or watches, or chance the dangers of the park at night. No one would do them any harm. They did not walk down stairs without a firm grip on the banisters. Dear God, what stagnant lives they led.

But her parents were shoreline zoologists who never could resist the chance of poking about in the tides and shallows of the coast. Syl had spent a solitary childhood on the shore, bored with a picnic and a book, praying for beach games, sandcastles and other girls, while Joseph and Celice had rummaged in the water, crying out – so annoyingly – whenever they discovered a rare weed or felt the sand beneath their feet palpitate with some shy fish.

Oddly, they'd never taken her to the Baritone coast in all their years of beachcombing. Her mother had not liked that stretch. But all the other shores and bays, the Mu, the Horseman Rocks, Tiger Crab Bay, Cape Shoals were chillingly familiar and frightening. She'd not forgotten the first time that she'd stood, aged eight, the beach's only castaway, to watch the panavision of her tiny parents washed out by the widest tide, their footings gone, their arms held up for help.

Too often they had overstayed the welcome of the sea and

were left stranded on a bar or chevronned by the waves or caught by muscular and unrelenting tides. She'd had to witness from the sand, the shingle or the rocks their minutes of exquisite panic while they forged a chest-deep route around the current or flailed between the reefs. Syl well remembered sitting once with her mother in the dilapidated ribs of an abandoned fishing boat while Father was out 'sifting' in his waist boots. Her mother said, 'He's too far out!' and started calling, 'Joseph! Joseph!' The tide had turned and her father, struggling against the heavily backing water and its tumbling undertow, had lost his balance. Her mother was half-way down the beach and Syl was crying, an already broken-hearted little girl, a hater of the sea, before her father struggled to his feet again. Then he was floating. They could see his boots, like two seal heads. They had to leave it to the waves to bring him in. Thank heavens it was a rising tide. He came ashore, soaked to the skin. He stood spitting sea-water and coughing while her mother screamed at him, 'You could have drowned! Then what?'

Syl had been ashamed to catch herself wondering how her friends would have reacted if Father had been killed. She'd be the centre of attention for a term. She'd have time off school. Everyone would treat her like a sick princess. She'd have to have a hat to wear at Father's funeral. Their empty house would fill up with relatives and neighbours. Maybe the uncle from America would come. She'd have the noise and fuss she'd always hankered for. But not from her father.

It was not difficult, then, now that Baritone Bay was in her sights, for Syl to picture all the details of her parents' deaths. Theirs was a comeuppance earned, deserved, by thirty years of paddling. She could imagine how her mother had run down the beach again, tossing his name out across the water as if it were a lifebelt: 'Joseph! Joseph!' Her father – older now and not as fit – had disappeared. Weighed down, perhaps, by heavy boots which, once they filled with water, were like leaden legs. He had not surfaced when the legendary seventh wave had hit him. Celice had stood – Syl put her there – with the water at her feet, studying the sea, waiting for it to reveal the sodden shadow of a struggling man, a bobbing head, an arm, a boot. The sea was shadowless for far too long. Her mother would have paddled in up to her knees. Then, perhaps, she might have seen his body rolling in the breakers like a log or else she might have heard a sinking call, half gull, half man. And so she'd waded in up to her thighs, her chest, her chin. She'd gone too deep herself. She might even have reached and touched his clothes. She could have caught hold of his arm and tried to pull him to the beach. But they were being tugged by weed and he was wet and heavy. He'd pulled her under with him. Her feet were well clear of the sand. For once her height and weight were not a help. The seaweed could not carry her. She dared not let him go and try to save herself. Now there was no one on the beach to rescue them. No little girl. All that remained was for the bodies to be carried out and back, for a tide or two, until a high and kindly sea had tossed them on the shore at Baritone Bay and rolled them to the edges of the dunes for dogs to find. Syl could expect, once she had walked to Baritone Bay, to find their bodies bloated by sea-water, draped in weed, their hands and faces grazed by sand, and bruised by all the ocean's buffeting.

Syl wasn't really dressed for walking. She'd thrown on the

same clothes that she'd been wearing the day before at the morgue: a concert shirt, black jodhpur leggings, slip-on shopping shoes. In the car she had been uncomfortably hot. Now, with still a couple of kilometres to walk before she reached the bay she was beginning to regret that she had not paused to find one of her mother's jackets and a stouter pair of shoes before she'd left her parents' home. The sea breeze had a chilling edge to it and she was shaking uncontrollably. She clasped her arms around herself, clutching her elbows with the opposing hands, and hurried along the coastal track. She looked as if she'd just popped out for bread.

She might have shivered anyway, even if she had been dressed for winter, even if the day were sunny, even if the policewoman who was now discreetly trailing her had done what she was tempted to and taken off her uniform jacket to lend to her odd charge. After all, Syl was expecting to encounter death, and death is cold and damp. She should expect the temperatures to drop the closer she got to the place where her parents had been found. That's why churches are so cold. That's why the snow in graveyards seems to last much longer than the snow in streets. That's why the northern conifer does well in cemeteries. That's why you have to wear an overcoat and dress in black even for a summer funeral. The grave yawns Arctic air.

Syl had not paid much attention when the woman officer had said, 'We have a policy at any scene of a crime.' But as she walked, concentrating now on the path and trying not to notice the Salt Pines stretch of coast, the spreading sky, the sea complicit with the sands in its damp shades, the words popped back into her mind. The 'scene of crime'. What crime?

She hadn't thought there'd been a crime except, perhaps, the taking of her parents' car by some soft, opportunist teenager who couldn't find a taxi fare; and the theft of a radio. She hadn't dreamed or feared a crime. She'd feared the logic of the sea. She'd dreamed their classic executioner was Fish.

Her escort crossed the gap and joined her when they reached the narrow path that left the coastal track and led into the dunes. The police had marked a route with canes and paper flags. The two women had to follow it exactly. It took them round the outside of the dunes, across the headland rocks and then, a sharp left-angle, inland, on wooden boards.

Syl had not expected so many policemen. She'd hardly ever seen as many in one place, except at riots on the television or at parades. There was a group in forage uniforms spread about amongst the dunes, searching every clump of grass, turning over every piece of drift. There were civilian attendants talking into mobile phones, and forensic investigators, wearing protective cotton overalls and gloves.

Nor had she imagined that there'd be a tent. A small marquee, in fact. Thick green canvas with the city's logo stamped on its side. At first Syl took it to be a catering tent for the policemen, the sort she'd seen at fairs, sports events and town carnivals. It was, she quickly realized, sheltering the bodies. And protecting the 'scene of crime'. Syl hugged her elbows tightly. She and her escort were the only living women there.

'Where are they?' Syl asked the policewoman, wanting confirmation.

'They're coming.'

'I mean my parents!' The answer froze her to the bone.

'Inside,' she said. 'The tent. You have to wait. They're making them presentable.'

Syl was suddenly so faint and breathless that she had to sit down on the lissom grass, her back to the tent, and look for comfort in the dunes. There was none. A police photographer was taking pictures of a torn white shirt stretched out like a flag in the branches of a thornbush. She sat as still as possible, so still that she could feel her heartbeat in her toes.

At last a man her father's age came out of the tent, holding a purple sacados and a cardboard box. 'Recognize this?' he asked. No introductions or formalities. Syl shook her head at the blackening blood prints on its leather shoulder strap. 'Or these?' A pair of women's shoes. Again she shook her head. 'The phone?' He held up a clear plastic bag with a black mobile phone inside.

She peered at it. 'I couldn't say,' she said. 'They're all the same.'

'Is that your parents' number?' He pulled the plastic tight and pointed to the line of digits written on the tag.

'I can't remember,' she said. 'That is my father's handwriting, though. He does his fives like that.'

'Or this?' A rain-soaked copy of the *Entomology*, bloodstained.

'They did subscribe.'

He didn't show her the granite club they'd found, tossed in the grass and almost picked clean of the blood and human tissue by the crabs and flies, though he was tempted. He didn't mind the public face of grief and shock. It was reassuring and appropriate. He was not one of the new school who considered mourning and weeping little better than masturbation. A daughter, in circumstances such as this, ought to be hysterical.

*His* daughter would be, he hoped. It was her right. It was her duty. This woman, though, was far too sensible and rational. Too furtive and controlled. Too studenty and cropped. Too underdressed for such a solemn task.

'OK, let's have a look inside,' he said, taking her arm. 'Hold on to me.'

'No thanks.' She was used to such men, from her waitressing. She pulled her arm free, and stepped a pace away. Once he had turned his back on her, she followed him into the tent. The usual canvas smells were absent. There was no scent of cloth or waterproofing, just the odours of damp grass, with iodine, formaldehyde, and sweat. Any daylight that succeeded in penetrating the canvas was thin, green and ghostly.

It was warm inside. Out of the wind. There were four younger men already there, olive-faced and business-like. The older one who'd summoned her just said, 'The daughter,' then, 'The lights.' Two hanging fluorescent lamps stuttered into life for a few moments then shed their hard sheen on to a spread of improbably long white sheets laid out on the sloping grass inside the tent at Syl's feet. The beds of sloping lissom grass seemed dulled now that the ghostly green had been supplanted by mechanical light.

'It's only the faces,' the detective said. 'We'll make it very quick. Just nod. Or shake your head. We'll do the woman first.' He bent and turned back the top sheet and the refrigerating blanket, put there to keep the bodies cold and fresh. Celice.

Syl had only an instant's view. It was her mother, much reduced, but unmistakable. Her face was cheek down, turned sideways, resting on the pillow of the grass. Her mouth was swollen and her skull collapsed. Her best front teeth were grinning, cracked from root to tip. Her skin was indigo. The hair was dappled with dead blood.

'Just nod or shake your head,' he said again.

'It's her.'

'And now the man, if you're ready?' He knelt on the grass further down the array of sheets, looking at Syl, waiting for her to compose herself, hoping for some high response.

She was composed. She felt relieved, in fact. The pressure was reduced. Nothing could be worse than this, so there was nothing more to fear. 'I want to see it all,' she said. 'Not just the face. Take all the sheets away.' He did so at once, pulling the sheets and refrigerating blankets up towards himself and gathering them against his chest. She nodded twice. Then shook her head in disbelief. The doctors of zoology. The lost and secret couple, Joseph and Celice, on their sixth day of grace. At last, the mystery. At last, the solace of the world's worst thing.

A trained mortician or pathologist, used to the pus and debris of exploded tissue, the ruptured membranes leaking lymph, the killing fields of murdered cells, might find a thousand signs of disassembly and decay on Joseph and Celice's cadavers. Their eyeballs were already liquefying and their faces were enlarged. Their skin was blistered on the undersides. Their innards were so bloated from the by-products of decomposition – methane and ethium – that their nostrils, ears and open wounds had been made frothy by exuding gas.

But at the distance that their daughter viewed them from, in that exaggerated light, they seemed less troubled than they had even that morning when they'd been found in natural light. Except for the typical glaucous bruises above the small intestine, their livid colours had calmed down, more blue than purple, more grey than green. They had even tanned and darkened a little in the sun. And the hours of rigor mortis had long passed. Their arms and legs no longer stuck out like mannequins. Joseph's one wild sign, death's unkind erection, had reduced. Their bodies were unstiffened and fell into the hollows of the grass, like sleepers fall into the cushions of a bed, relaxed and rounded, fitting in.

The crabs had gone. Celice and Joseph were not fresh enough for them. And though the swag flies had deposited more eggs in the couple's open cavities, most of the flies had now departed, kept away first by the covering of wind-borne sand that was embalming Joseph and Celice and then by the busy presence of the police. The forensic officers had hoovered out the maggots, 'making them presentable', before the daughter came.

Syl was too touched by the gentle nakedness and disposition of her parents to stop herself from sobbing. Sobbing on the edges of the sea as she had so many times before when Joseph and Celice were too far out to reach. The policewoman who had been standing outside was summoned. A job at last. She put her coat round Syl's shoulders and laid her arm too heavily across her back.

The body sheets had been pulled across again without Syl noticing, but she had got a snapshot printed in her mind. She'd not remember all the wounds, the gull damage, the black dry blood. It was her father's hand wrapped round her mother's leg that haunted and delighted her. It looked as if the leg and arm were keeping them earthbound.

'They didn't drown?'

'That's right, they didn't drown,' the detective said. 'Somebody with a rock.'

'A murderer?'

A nod.

'Who, then?'

The policeman shrugged. He meant, Maybe we'll never know.

'You've no idea?' insisted Syl. 'Do say!'

'Mondazy's Fish,' he said – the old phrase, meaning Fate. The usual crap.

'Show me their faces one last time. I'll be OK.'

Her parents seemed oddly young and flourishing, in this second, edited glimpse of them, through half-shut eyes. Their skin was stretched. Her father's forehead was unlined. Her mother's underchin was firm. But there was something else that made them young, Syl realized. The very manner of their deaths. For violent death is usually the province of the young. Slow wasting is the property of age. And there was none of that. They were, indeed, quite handsome in their fast dilapidation; despite the damage and the wounds, they had not surrendered any of their nature or their character. They'd not depersonalized. They were uplifting in their way, and oddly calm. Here was a suicide of sorts, because her parents had escaped those last, geriatric shudders – convulsions was too strong a word – which dog a person from the womb. Yet this was also something happier than suicide. No evidence of anger, sorrow or despair. No farewell note. No self-inflicted wounds. No legacy of spite. No last regrets. They had departed from their world while there was still good health to keep them sweet and their old age to look forward to with hope.

Syl had to allow them this at least: her parents had surprised her this one time. Not just their murder. Nor their nakedness. But that they had the power, on their deaths, to flush her heart – too late – with love. It was the light touch of his finger on her leg.

'Don't move my father's hand,' she said.

Syl could not arrange the funeral at once, and flee the coast, as she would have liked. The bodies, according to the detective, would have to stay inside the tent until the Monday. Forensics had to do their work and the police preferred to keep the corpses where they were until they'd checked each grain of sand, each blade of grass for clues. Then the magistrate would need to come to issue a certificate of removal. It all took time. And magistrates are not at work on Sundays. So Syl, instead, asked Geo to drop her at the Mission Church at the harbour in the town centre. No need to wait for her, she said. She didn't know how long she'd be. She'd make her own way home. A slim excuse for getting rid of him. Her parents had been married at this church and Celice had always said that it would be a happy final resting-place. Syl needed time alone. She would light a candle, sit in semi-darkness and concentrate on what their deaths might mean.

The Mission Church was busy with a service when she arrived, so she sat outside on the commemorative benches made from the timbers of wrecked ships and carved with the names of lost seamen and waited for the worshippers to leave. The world went on. It orbited through space. There were the usual markers of the day. A sinking sky. The sound of motor-cars. The muted Sunday clatter of the port. And, finally, the sound of people singing hymns, their voices raised against the universe, as thin as water and as nourishing.

It wasn't difficult for Syl, with that accompaniment, to recall the image of her parents, side by side and murdered on a bed of grass, her ankle in his hand. She tried to let the hymning voices pick up the bodies from the dunes and take them to the kingdom of their verses, amongst the heavens and eternities, into the everlasting peace. But it was obvious that these were voices and these were verses that had not got the muscle to displace a single leaf, let alone pass sinners into paradise. Her father's songs, for all their mawkish sentiment, were far more powerful. Love songs transcend, transport, because there's such a thing as love. But hymns and prayers have feeble tunes because there are no gods.

By the time the worshippers were coming out, Syl had lost her need for solitude and candles. She walked away, a member of the parting congregation, euphoric and dismayed at once, and only praying that her life would have as much love as her parents' had.

Syl had not asked herself the greater question yet. She was too young to need the death-defying trick of living in a godless and expanding universe, its gravity dispersing by the second, its spaces stretching and unspannable, its matter darkening. Life is. It goes. It does not count. That was the hurtling truth that comes to rattle everyone as they grow up, grow old. Syl need not worry for a while.

But she had at least an answer to the lesser question. How should the dying spend their time when life's short portion shrinks with every waking day? She'd walked to see mortality that Sunday afternoon and found her parents irredeemable.

Her gene suppliers had closed shop. Their daughter was the next in line. She could not duck out of the queue. So she should not waste her time in this black universe. The world's small, breathing denizens, its quaking congregations and its stargazers, were fools to sacrifice the flaring briefness of their lives in hopes of paradise or fears of hell. No one transcends. There is no future and no past. There is no remedy for death – or birth – except to hug the spaces in between. Live loud. Live wide. Live tall.

She could not ape her parents' life. She would not merely turn her back against the coffin-hurtling streets and focus only on the minutes in the room, the light that makes an oval of the square, the half-filled diary open at the week, the music on the stereo, the kettle heating on the stove, the photos poked between the mirror and its frame, the dancing page, the other person breathing in a chair, still life. She would, instead, embrace the warmer fevers of the world. Their deaths were her beginning.

These have been unusual days, she thought, as she walked back towards the empty house, her house, through first the wide catalpa-lined avenues of the centre then the gaunt, less pungent streets of the inner suburbs. I am bereaved and liberated at one stroke (a dozen blows). There isn't anything beyond me now. There isn't anything I cannot think about, or say.

She would make plans. Bright days ahead.

# 21

Joseph was out of bed early on the morning of his death. He was always up before Celice. He took his breakfast out to the greying, sapwood deck behind the house, and found just sufficient space for his chair in that trapezium of light where the first sun of the day, if there were any, stretched across the boards. This was where his own father, twenty years before and sitting in the same sunlight, had been killed by a stroke, and where, a thousand times when she was small, his daughter had climbed on to her father's lap, her bony bottom on his bony knee, to beg for breakfast from his tray, and a song. Syl loved to listen to him saying things in song, in his mad, comic bass, that he could never say in life. Those were the only times he made her laugh.

The condemned man did not eat much. He was the supper not the breakfast sort. He had vanilla coffee on that day, some mango and a cheese brioche, too stale to finish. He'd arranged the food – together with a peeling-knife, his Cardica pills, his daily ledger and a pen – on a featherwood tray as neatly as an airline meal, as if he needed to remind himself of his sparing moderation and his discernment, his high blood pressure hardly helped by all the coffee that he drank, his growing singleness. He exercised his finger joints, battled with his morning cough, waited for his head to clear. He was, as usual, tired.

But not even Joseph could fail to be diverted by the sun. The radio had promised fine weather for a change. He'd make the most of it. Many people in the town on that day would make the most of it. They would invent aching backs and flu, sudden funerals to attend or urgent business somewhere away from their desks and yards so that they could reward themselves with a dry day or two off work. The parks and public lawns could be their offices. The restaurants would be packed out.

We know exactly what Joseph did. He phoned the Institute at 7.25 a.m. and left a message for his secretary on their answerphone. He had some fieldwork to complete, he said, and would not come into his office until early Thursday morning. She could telephone him on the mobile if she needed to, but only 'urgent things'. This was his final contact with the world at large, the last time that his voice was heard. He'd started off the day by telling lies. He felt both nervous and excited. He wrote a one-line, optimistic entry in his ledger and, warming in the sun, imagined how he and his wife might pass the day.

Once he had dressed, showered and succumbed to a second coffee, Joseph took a glass of tea and a dish of sliced fruit to Celice in her bed. A tender treat? An uncomplicated invitation to the pleasures of the sun? No, he hoped to give her more than breakfast. His breathing was already thin and papery with desire for her. A little lie, a little sun, some mango and a pill, an overdose of caffeine, an unexpected holiday is all it takes to make a man feel amorous.

Their rooms were separate and had been for more than twenty years, since Syl was born in fact and had demanded a share of her mother's pillow every night. Even when Syl was a teenager Joseph had not returned to Celice's bed for sleep. He said it was because he did not like the smell of her tobacco, but did not want to spoil the pleasure that she took in a breakfast cigarette. He hadn't gone back to the room four months before when she had given up her smoking, though. Privately, they both acknowledged that they had become too shy and selfish to accommodate the patterns of each other's sleep, or tolerate a squeaking bed, or share the coverlet.

Occasionally, now that Syl had gone away (to lead – and waste – her own life, doing God-knows-what) Joseph went into his wife's room in the evening, into her bed, but always left when she had gone to sleep. Celice required eight hours every night. She was making up for all the sleep she'd missed when she was young. Any less and she would be irascible all day. Joseph still only needed five or six hours, and he slept creakily, breathing like a dog, stretching, stumbling to the lavatory by moonlight four, five times a night. Sometimes he sat up wide awake at two or three o'clock, and read a further chapter of a book. He could never sleep if it was raining or if some merchant liner, idling in the fog, was sounding warnings on its horn. Once in a while he didn't go to bed at all but stayed up with the bottle of Negrita gleewater he kept hidden on a kitchen shelf and a pack of cards, and listened to the radio on headphones. Lectures, news, debates. Not music, unless there was a recital of sentimental songs. He did not share his wife's passion for the orchestra. Syl's parents, her father and *maman*, were not compatible in bed or in the concert hall. Celice went to the concert hall and bed alone.

He must have hesitated, surely, when he stood and watched her sleeping, her ears still stuffed with cotton plugs, her eyes encrusted with the spongy detritus of sleep, her hair in tufts. She still looked tired. She was not yet the wife of his imagination, alert, sweet-smelling, crisply dressed, available. He knew she had no classes to teach on a Tuesday or a Wednesday and usually would choose to sleep till noon on her days off, happy to wake to an empty house, glad to have a spinster day. It was so tempting, though, to reach out and touch, or even to let drop his clothes and climb into the bed with her. But he was sensible, of course. He was a doctor of zoology and over fifty years of age. He knew he ought to let her sleep and tiptoe from the room. Perhaps he should drive off somewhere to enjoy the sun all on his own. She'd never know. She'd think he was at work as usual. He could do exactly what he wanted. That was – for a moment – his sun-fuelled fantasy. Go to a bar. Go to a show. Go to a prostitute – he'd like to pay for sex, just once, before he died. Sit out beneath the trees in Almanac Square while some young woman served him fish and vegetables, her body within reach. He could be foolish for a change. Be young for once.

Fat chance of that.

He coughed to wake her up, and to reawaken himself. He put her tea and breakfast on the bedside table. He placed her bookmark in her open book. He picked up a crumpled tissue and pushed it back beneath her pillow. He rescued her watch from the floor and laid it on the dressing-table – somewhere safe and visible where she would find it easily. Here was the splendid truth that so many men discover far too late, but he had known for years. He could be young and foolish only with his wife.

Joseph considered that it might be best to let her sleep till nine o'clock. She'd not complain at that. Or he could let the sunlight waken her, perhaps. He pulled the cord on the blinds so that they parted by a couple of centimetres. The streaming slats of sun, sliced into patterns by the blinds, spread across the cover of her bed in undulating bands. She did not wake, not even when he opened the blinds some centimetres more so that the light fell on her eyes. Her mouth dropped open and her wheezing nose was silenced, but still she slept.

Now he was anxious and impatient. Her tea would get cold. The weather would not last. Good fortune such as this is always fleeting. There would be clouds and mist ready to burst in on their day like spoiling boys. It was a waste (a phrase she hated) to let the day deteriorate while Celice slept. She would not thank him if he let her sleep through this.

Here was his plan. He should not be ashamed. They had some business on the coast. When they had read in the newspapers and seen in television reports that all the shorelands between the airport and Baritone Bay had been bought by a consortium of businessmen with plans for a holiday village and an estate of expensive houses their hearts had sunk. Here the rich would hide behind high walls and top their gates with barbed wire. The bankers and the businessmen would travel in and out, past guards, with the blinds down in their limousines. Think of the damage to the wildlife habitats, they said. The loss of beach and dunes.

But actually their discomfort was mostly at the loss of somewhere packed with memories, the good and bad. Celice feared the place, its chilling winds, its unremitting sea, its ever-smoky sky. Joseph had been there on several occasions during the marriage, though not recently. Not, in fact, for nineteen years. There'd been a period, though, when he was younger, when he'd got to know it well. Sometimes, when he'd had an afternoon to spare and no one knew, he'd drive out to the coast alone, self-consciously, as if he had a private rendezvous. He'd walk along the track with his binoculars, inspect the shore, but always end up in the dunes, remembering, reliving if he could, his seduction by Celice. That startling day. That *once*. Those transformations on the beach.

He'd always wanted to return with her. Of course. The first encounters are the best. 'Let's go out to the bay,' he'd suggested a thousand times, 'for old times' sake. Before we die.' But she had not agreed, not once. She didn't even like to reminisce in too much detail about the week when she and Joseph had met, their lovemaking – because to think about that week was to remind herself of Festa and the fire, how passion could be murderous, how love could set the flame. She'd blamed herself for almost thirty years, no matter what Joseph had to say: 'Be rational, forget the past'; 'It's my fault just as much as yours'; 'A fire can start in hundreds of different ways.' He made no difference. Celice hoped never to have to go back there again.

But once the plans for Salt Pines had been printed in the newspaper – and once she'd heard about the Academic Mentor's suicide – *never* became too real a word for her. Up to that point she'd had the choice to stay away, but once Salt Pines was constructed with its protected gates the choice would be removed. Perhaps the time had come to take control of what she might be guilty of, and not be ruled by it. She said to Joseph, lightly, as she left for work one day so that he wouldn't have the chance to lecture her, 'Maybe we ought to go out there. I think we ought to go. Before they build.' He knew she only meant that they ought to see the burnt remains of the study house, to put Festa's ghost to rest before the bulldozers erased the place where she'd died. A resurrection in the dunes was not part of her plan.

But Joseph lent a sympathetic pair of ears, for once. Of course, she should return and face the past, he said, while she pulled on her coat. He'd been saying so for years. But when he pictured it – as he would a dozen times a day in the ensuing weeks – he did not visualize them standing on a blackened wall throwing flowers where once there'd been a long veranda and Festa sleeping. Instead, he placed himself and Celice, young and naked, in the dunes, her shocking fingers pulling at his clothes. This Tuesday, with its rare sunshine, would be the perfect opportunity to lead his wife down from the study house again to the hidden chambers of the shore. He'd have to be discreet, of course. Their only stated plan could be a return to the scorched remains. But then, when that was done, he could suggest a hunt for sprayhoppers, perhaps. And then a picnic. Somewhere with soft grass, private and protected from the wind.

He took her hand and squeezed the fingers. Waking her was making love to her. 'Celice, it's warm,' he said. 'Too good to waste. Are you awake? Celice. Let's make the most of it.' He knew better than to shake her. She would already be annoyed with him. This was her room. This was her day. If she was touched again or shaken, she had the right to pinch the thin flesh on his arm. She was a worshipper of sleep and orchestras.

Finally she opened an eye to squint at him. Her husband was a shining, haloed silhouette. His body half obscured the sun. 'What's wrong?' she asked. Her voice had hardly changed in thirty years.

'Come on, let's make the most of it. It's such a waste,' he said again, as if she hadn't already heard his aggravating little phrase. 'Sit up. There's tea. It's warm outside.'

'It's warm in here.'

This, he knew, was not an invitation to get in. He wanted her to sit up in the bed. He hoped that if she did, she might stretch her arms, straight out from her shoulders in a crucifixion mime and make a little strangulated cry, a seagull yawn, to wake herself and clear her throat. Her nightdress sleeves were always loose – she did not like the claustrophobia of hugging clothes – and Joseph knew that when she stretched she'd make an open, hanging corridor of cloth below her arm for anyone to hold their breath and view her snubby breasts. He'd seen her do exactly that so many times before. He'd learned the trick of waiting with her breakfast at the bedroom door and calling her name. Sex was so underhand. He knew exactly where to stand to catch the light. She'd wake and stretch her unsuspecting arms for him. She did not disappoint him now. Stolen glimpses of his wife.

So there was Joseph on the morning of his death, flushed already by the early sun and by the prospect of an outing with Celice, looking down along the cotton and the flesh towards the hollows and the beacons of her armpits and her chest, her blemishes, her moles, the rib bones of a woman thin with age, the smell of her – bedclothes and sweat – the smell of breakfast on a tray, her body sliced up by the sun into jagged bands of shade and light. He must have wanted there and then to pass his body down the sleeve and press his lips into her shadows and her silhouettes. He'd have to wait.

# 22

Baritone Bay and its backdunes were never popular with townies. That's why the campaign to prevent the building of Salt Pines was bound to fail. Who cared about this odd and unattractive coast? The swimming there was dangerous: cross-tides and undertows. The winds were unpredictable. Either they were bursting from the sea, wet, salt-laden, cold, uncomfortable, or they were twisting with the contours of the coast to sandblast anybody mad enough to picnic on the shore or take their sweaters off. Even walkers kept away. Why make the detour over boulders, pebbles and dunes when the earth-packed coastal path was more direct and prettier? Families and swimmers would rather drive out to the city beach the other side of town, where there were strings of scalloped coves, soft sands, lifeguards, some timber restaurants and an attendant forest of cool pines where they could park their cars, ride bikes and horses, erect their tents, and light their barbecues. And where, of course, the only sounds were of people having fun.

In recent years even the peace and quiet of Baritone – its one undisputed attraction – had been destroyed by advances at the airport. Now there were jumbos coming in and out each day across the coast, and scatty little jets. They'd opened up a private field, for businessmen and amateurs. At weekends leisure pilots made a nuisance of themselves daredevilling the ocean and the sands. The spoilt and wealthy residents of Salt

Pines would need tree screens and muffler windows or nerves of steel. The guards, the gatehouse and high walls could not keep out the din of aircraft.

But before the extensions to the runways in the early nineties the only passenger planes that could get in were Stols and Trilanders, light-bodied craft that needed only two hundred metres to take off, and less to land. The coast was quieter then.

Nevertheless, the rumbling that Joseph and Celice could hear, that morning almost thirty years ago when they crept from the study house for their first tryst, must be, they thought, a plane, a low and heavy one. And one so close to them as they walked out across the shore, the sprayhoppers flying at their feet, their footprints belching air and water in their wake, that its roaring engines seemed to come out of the dunes. They tried to spot some movement in the clouds, the tell-tale, sleepless winking of the plane's red eyes. The grey straight ruler of a wing. They turned their heads and whirled about in the shallows to fix co-ordinates of sound and find the source of that low noise.

The plane did not pass over them. It stayed and grumbled in the dunes. Its engines idled, then picked up and roared again whenever there was any wind. The nearer that Celice and Joseph got to the jutting foreland of the bay the louder it became. Of course, they realized quite soon what they were witnessing. Not an aeroplane. It was the celebrated baritone, the voice that everybody said could bring bad luck. Someone'll die. There'll be a month of gales and rain. There'll be a ghost.

Celice and Joseph were bombarded by a hundred sounds. The deeper that they got into the dunes the less the roar resembled aircraft engines and the more it shaped itself like fire or hymns or thunder. Each step produced new scenes. First there was a furnace blast, and then the foghorn of a grounded ship, a sonic boom too soon for superjets, a pair of warring clouds. Finally the air drift picked up speed and steadied long enough for the sound that gave the bay its name to settle in – the humming fugue of men in churches, exercising their voices before a funeral or tuning up their instruments, choir practice from an organ loft. Celice and Joseph thought the sea was booming, that the baritone was coming off the tide, but when they climbed a dune peak to look, the sea was flat and quiet. Yet the higher they climbed the louder were the notes, and every time the wind picked up the lower was the compass of the song. This was the baritone of mourning and of saxhorns, sepulchral, pessimistic, deep. If they'd had any sense, if they had been less scientific and self-occupied, they would have run, as any small child would. They would have run upwind across the open shore and then uphill towards the safety of the study house to wrap their sleeping-bags around their ears.

But Joseph and Celice were scientists in love. They would not run away, with superstition at their heels. Their hearts were set on lesser things. They knew it would not be a grand enough response to crooning landscapes just to say, as *almost* doctors of zoology should feel obliged to say, 'There is a natural explanation for the voices that we hear. There's no such thing' – that reassuring phrase again – 'as bad luck in a natural world'. But they thought it just the same. The baritone might be a proper subject for scientific study, but it was not unnatural. They were not the types, even in their current, heightened mood, to be impressed or daunted by the portent readers and the phenomenologists who made false patterns out of chaos, who said, for instance, 'If there's a heavy dew tonight, there'll be fine weather in the morning.' Or, 'When the sapnut trees are cropping heavily it means the coming winter will be punishing, hard winds, long storms, deep frosts.' Or that expressions on the face of the moon presaged the fortunes of the infants born that night. A frowning moon would produce a class of melancholic kids. Or that the baritone meant death or gales or ghosts.

Our doctors of zoology or anybody who understands the mundane manners of the world, its rigid, sequenced protocols, would counter with the dulling truth that dew, sapnuts, the faces of the moon, can only show conditions that have passed. The earth is not a visionary and can't be blamed for what's ahead. It is retrospective, like the lovers would become, in those long years before the two of them were dead and dying in this place, before they were required to pay a heavy price for their nostalgia. It is the past that shapes the world. The future can't be found in it. So heavy dews will indicate only that the sky has been clear and conditions favourable for the deposition of dew. A glut of sapnuts is a sign of nothing more than that the preceding spring and summer were good for *Juglans suca* trees. And so it is with singing salt dunes. They do not predict the fast-advancing misfortunes of the world. They merely say, 'Conditions are correct for singing.'

And so it was that morning for Joseph and Celice. Conditions were correct for singing, that is all. The sand was still a little moist from sea spray, dust free and already warmed above 16° centigrade by the sun and by the heat retained from the previous day's fine weather. The surface sand grains on the dune slopes were well rounded, as required, and coated with a layer of silica – otherwise this would have been known as Tone Deaf Bay, not Baritone, producing a cacophony of frequencies and not the coherent and acoustic wave of singing. There was, as well, the optimum direction and velocity of wind. And there had been a catalyst, someone, some fleeting thing, a gull, a fox, a slipping dune, to start the salt sand moving and allow the famous baritone to croon. The singing only signified the scientific present and its past.

But Joseph and Celice were becoming less scientific by the minute. They were becoming more disposed to take the baritone not as a sign of bad luck but as a blessing. They would not say the earth had moved for them, but they could claim that the landscape had broken out in song and was arousing them, and was embracing them.

They had, in fact, not even touched each other so far that morning. He'd seen her almost naked through the veranda windows and had been terrified. She'd pulled her nightshirt high above her head. There were three sudden triangles of hair, her armpits and her crotch, and then the dropping of her head hair, springing back in place as the shirt's tight neckband cleared her forehead. She'd turned away before he had a chance to see her breasts. He'd caught an instant only of her narrow waist, her perfect eighteenth-century back, the age of flesh and dimples. She'd bent to pick the clothes out of a drawer. Then her body disappeared again, beneath a modest working shirt, and she became the wader on one leg pulling on a pair of pants, her socks, blue jeans, black jumper, walking boots. She'd turned and waved at him. He'd never been so shocked or fearful. He was a small boy at the blind summit of a roller-coaster ride, poised at the limits of control, his stomach in his mouth, and no retreat.

He had not dared to take her hand as they'd walked down to Baritone Bay. One fingertip, one uninvited touch, and she would disappear, he thought. And she had not attempted to touch him either. Touch is too obvious. She walked ahead. She let her body swing. She let him watch. She knew she was the centre of his universe. She wanted, if she could, to leave this small man giddy. He'd have a heart-attack. The earth would swallow him. He'd have a fit and bite his tongue in half. He would be speechless when she'd done with him.

Celice only touched him when they'd topped the outer dune to listen to the ululating orchestra of sand. She knew she'd have to overcome his nervousness and inexperience. She had to take command. She stood behind him and let the tumbling sand beneath their feet topple them together. She put both hands on his hips as if to steady herself. Quite innocent. Quite sisterly. But then she pressed her chin and mouth against his head and smelt the musty mushroom of his scalp. The sudden pressure seemed to clear his lungs of oxygen. He gasped and buckled under her, a man with just one bone. She had to hold him round the waist to stop him falling. Her fingers dug into his clothes, first at the side and then around his abdomen. She pulled up his shirt, $T = \frac{50n-40}{4}$, and found the space between his belt and navel. Room enough for her slim wrist.

He winced, and shook. He doubled up. 'Cold hands,' he said.

'Good pastry,' she replied.

Joseph was indeed sent giddy. He pressed his back into Celice's chest. He turned his face towards her. An awkward angle. His mouth was lifted, open, pink. He was a greedy little bird. She fed him fat worms with her tongue. She had to duck her knees and tip her head to find his mouth with hers.

The lissom grass was irresistible, the perfect blanket, velvety and sensuous. Celice and Joseph fell on their knees and pulled each other's trousers down. She stretched her toes beyond his toes when they made love. She liked her Joseph all the more for being small. She liked to be the wrapper, not the wrapped. And he was clearly more than happy to be eclipsed by her, to have his light shut out by her descending shapes, to have his breathing blocked, his ears absorbed into her mouth, to earn the wet and grateful puppy kiss across his fingertips when finally he dared to touch between her legs.

No one could say their love was cautious. Love on that day was bold. Joseph was not as reckless as she'd hoped he'd be. But she enjoyed his shaking passion and the way – once he had found his voice – he glorified the parts of her he liked, the wonder of her springy hair, the girlish, modest chest, the way her skin was coloured in its contours, summit white but darker in its crevices, at her throat, her armpits, under her breasts, her torso, the inside of her thighs. She showed him where to linger and what to leave alone. He even rubbed her back and neck, and kissed, as she requested, every vertebra. But still he was no maestro of the spine. Nor was he in control of her. It can't have helped that he was trembling with desire and that his senses of timing, balance and direction had deserted him. Or that he was attempting to make love to her still shackled by his underclothes and jeans. She should have guessed how green he'd be, how inexperienced, how lacking in technique. He was not the Casanova of her dreams. It was, though, thrilling to imagine what he might achieve when he became her lover, night on night, when he had learned to direct his energies more accurately. This first time, though, she'd do her best for him. She'd sacrifice herself.

It didn't matter, so he said, that after all her scheming and attention, his climax when it arrived was not a mighty one and hers was oddly short and shadowy, approaching and departing in one move. A shiver and a shudder; they were done. But were they satisfied? Entirely so. Not Eros manifest, perhaps. Not sent sublime by orgasms into the whirlpool of amnesia that poets claim – although it isn't true – is like the absolute forgetfulness of death. But happy to their fingertips. And pacified. And sparkling. And more in love – it's all that counts when all is said and done – than they had been before the sex.

There must have been a moment when the baritone stopped singing. The salt dunes did not make acoustic waves all morning. Conditions changed. The wind came round and dropped. The perfect angle was reduced. The sand dried out. The lovers did not care or even notice, though. They were not listening to the reverberations of the land, but to their own.

She wrapped herself around him afterwards. They were too deep to spot the distant, inland plume of smoke, or hear the calls of 'Joseph! Celice! Festa!' from the sprinting ornithologist. The dunes blocked out the world. They cuddled on the bed of lissom grass. They were the oddest pair, in their flat, hollow suntrap, hidden from the sea, with no idea of what the bay might have in store for them.

# 23

Syl was exhausted, naturally. It had been a day of walking. First along the coast and back. Then up from the Mission Church to the family house, a longer distance than she'd remembered from her childhood, but curative.

The town looked and smelt its best at dusk. The grime and wear became invisible. Man-made illuminations showed only the good parts of the streets. The coloured bar lights had come on, in all their ripening shades from green to red, no blues, like strings of mangoes. The pavement stalls, their wares side-lit by lanterns from the town's pre-electric past, were already trading Sunday treats: nut sticks, cocoa dips, candied fruit, doughnuts. The brochette salesmen raked the charcoal in their braziers. Each pulse of flame was their street cry. But, most of all, the dusk's illumination came from the headlamps of cars in swinging, lighthouse beams. The corridors of quizzing light retracted and stretched out to sweep the legs and faces of the people on the street. The sleeping Sunday town was resurrected in the evening. It was a time for families and lovers.

Syl would have gone into a bar or bought herself a cheese and pork brochette. She hadn't eaten anything that day. She'd had to leave for Baritone Bay before the ferryman had had a chance to bring the coffee and the cake he'd promised her for breakfast. And she was cold. Still just a shirt. No coat or jumper. A warm indoors, some food, a beer, some company were what she needed. Even the fall-short, underreaching comforts of a brazier would do. Or a speedy taxi ride back home. But she had not brought any money from the house, and hadn't had the nerve to borrow any from Geo. She'd have to starve. She'd have to walk. And she'd have to shiver all the way. A lively and romantic prospect, actually. It matched the way she felt about herself – an orphaned, independent woman, with empty pockets, empty stomach, cold and young, and passing through the bright and filling streets without a friend.

It wasn't long before Syl had left the Sunday carnival of crowds and lights. She crossed the river by the cycle bridge and followed the main boulevard out of the centre towards the hilltop houses where the artists, the academics and her parents lived. First there were the civic buildings, the pinkstone barracks and the regimental offices, the hotels of the Bankside district, the Geometric Gardens to hurry past. But then the streets were livelier again and Syl could peer down cul-de-sacs and into wayward tenements where students, conscripts, single men were dodging motorbikes and hesitating outside brothels, narrow bars and curtained doors, pretending to belong.

It was completely dark when Syl approached the railings of Deliverance Park. She had either to undertake the long walk round to reach the stretch of unmetalled side roads and the family house, or break a rule her parents had imposed since she was young and risk the night-time trespass and the trees. 'There isn't anything beyond me now,' she'd told herself, that afternoon, outside the Mission Church. 'There isn't anything I cannot do or say.' So she climbed the railings, dropped down on to the sodden plant beds and sprinted off into the dark, sprinted off as she had always wanted to, euphoric and untouchable. She let out great whoops of liberation and defeat as she progressed, as she was bound to, across safe lawns on to a pine-shielded path, blacker and more feverish than night, owl-eyed and loveless. Heading for the house that had to let her in.

The front door stuck even worse than usual. The opening was snagged by letters, cards, condolences, all hand-delivered during the day. Word had already got around. The murder was made public. Syl took them to the kitchen, put on the cooking-duty cardigan, which was left hanging, as ever, on the larder hook, and started hunting for her supper. There was – Sod's law – no food at home, except the breakfast cake, still lying on its plate and dried out by its hours of neglect. Nor was there any alcohol. Syl searched the kitchen cupboards again and her father's room, but all she found were a set of spirit glasses and the lees of some gleewater in a square bottle, half hidden on a high shelf, out of harm's way. Not worth the reach. The cake would have to do. She broke it into four dry pieces and started on the mail. Cards first, from neighbours mostly who hardly knew her parents. Photographs of clouds and aquatints of flowers with ornate fine lines from poets and the scriptures, being brave at the expense of death. 'Life is the Desert,' Syl was told in gold and silver italics. 'Death is the Rendezvous of Friends.' Or 'Death's a shadow, always at our heels.' Or, It's 'our second home. The feast is spread upon its table. The Host is waiting at its door.' Or 'Death's the veil which those who live call Life: They sleep and it is lifted.' Or (from the sepulchre in Milan where Claudio Busi, the architect, is buried) 'Death is nothing at all. I have slipped away into another room. All is well.' Except, thought Syl, that there's no slipping back.

The letters were all handwritten, from her parents' colleagues and the secretaries at the Institute and the university. *For Syl, For Sil, With love to Sylvia, For Celice and Joseph's daughter* ('Sorry, but we do not know your name'), *To Cyl.* All of them seemed fonder now of their two doctors of zoology than they had ever been in life. 'Your parents were admired by all of us,' they wrote. 'They were devoted. Anyone could tell. They will be missed. It's such a blessing, in a way, that they should have died in each other's arms.' And 'They are irreplaceable.'

It was as if Syl's parents' lives, which had seemed hidden and pale, illuminated by so few surface lights, at best a silhouette, only needed death's bright torch to bring the passion and the colour out. Its beam had caught and fixed them now. Their histories were certain. No more to come. No more to add. Their dates were written down indelibly. Nothing could be changed or mended, except by the sentiment and myth of those who were not dead. That's the only Judgement Day there is. The benefits of hindsight. The dead themselves are robbed of retrospect. They're not required to make sense of their deaths.

Syl dropped the letters and the cards in the waste-bin. She'd not reply. Life was too short. They'd understand. She gleaned the few cake crumbs off the table top with a wet finger. She stared out of the kitchen window at the dark and empty deck. She turned the taps on and off to check that the world was functioning. She was tired and hungry still and bored with home. It was not yet ten o'clock, but she would have to go to bed. What else was there to do?

She started in her mother's bed. She liked its space and the heavy coverlet. But it was unnerving to sink into the hollows of the mattress where the springs had been weakened by Celice and rest her head on pillows impacted by her mother's thousand nights and one. So she moved into her own room for the first time since that Friday night with Geo, and only for the second time in two years. These hollows were her own. It was like the simple legend on the condolence card, 'I have slipped away into another room. All is well.' Indeed. All would be well. She'd stay until the funeral, that day of chores and crowds, of false handshakes and noise. Then her parents could be dead in silence. And she could sell the house. She'd take the money and herself abroad, to all the places that she'd underlined in atlases when she was young, to Goa, Sydney, Rio, Rome, Berlin.

She was soon fast asleep. But not for long. Before eleven, she was woken by the same sound that she'd been half expecting on the previous night in this bed, the brakes and engine of her parents' car, their headlights flaring on her bedroom walls, their hurried steps up to the front door, the key, the tumbling of the locks, the cold reunions. All there that night. Except there was no tumbling of the locks. Someone had left the headlights of a car on full beam, shining at the front of the house. Someone was tapping on the door with the metal of a key. Syl pulled two slices of the window screen apart and looked down at the porch. It was the ferryman.

She went back to her bed and listened to him calling for her through the letterbox. A pretty sound, she thought. Syl, Syl. Syl, Syl. The sort of sound you'd make if you were stroking a cat. But she was never tempted to go down. She didn't want to be his cat. She'd slept with him three times already and she had more than paid her fare. She waited for his tapping to become less tentative, and then a hammering. His anger shook the house, but she was all the more unreachable. He would be certain she was there, inside and listening. He had, she knew, a right to be annoyed. She half expected pebbles at her window, a note wrapped round a stone; or to see his looming, rueful face pressed up against the window-glass. But he gave up quite quickly and drove away.

Again she was in Rio and she slept. The phone, which rang ten minutes after midnight, was not her parents getting through. She could not even dream they were alive. It was, of course, Geo again. The phone bell even had his plaintive ring. It wasn't hard to guess how he had passed the hour since he'd driven off. Either he was calling from the corner of a bar, enraged by drink and his unrewarded hankerings. Sex is the wasp trapped in the jar. Or he had gone back to his home – she'd never even asked him where he lived, but still with his parents, she was sure – and was sitting, sober and resentful, in their dark hallway, ready to beg and to berate when she picked up the phone: 'I thought I might come round,' and then, 'You thankless bitch.' She let it ring. And so did he. At last, she had to go downstairs to disconnect his call. She left the handset dangling. She'd be engaged all night.

Syl didn't try to sleep again. She'd had enough. She walked about the house, her mother's night-coat wrapped around her shoulders, and turned on every light, upstairs and down. Perhaps the lights would help her face the truth of her bereavement, and her guilt. She'd often daydreamed they were dead. And now they were. She still found satisfaction in their deaths

– they represented Goa and Berlin. She was to blame. For wanting it. For having too little love for them. For being less than they had hoped. For being thankless, lazy, hard.

She went again into her mother's room, pulled back the sheets and stared at the bed, looking for the trigger of some tears. She opened all the cupboards and the drawers, spread a hand across her mother's underclothes, inspected the unopened packet of cigarettes she found buried underneath, picked up her combs and necklaces, sniffed the cordite smell of hair on her brush, stared at the wedding photograph. But she felt nothing. Everything was too familiar. She opened Calvino's *Antonyms*. Her mother read the oddest things. And then the book that Syl herself had bought her father, *The Goatherd's Ancient Wisdom*. The book mark was a funeral card. A name she didn't recognize. The Academic Mentor at the university. 'Rejoice, for he has woken from his troubled dream,' it said. Another idiotic card. She dropped it, like she'd dropped the others, in the bin.

Her father's room was half the size, and cluttered. Again she pulled back the covers on the bed. A pair of patterned socks. And, pushed between the mattress and the footboard, there was a glossy magazine of photographs, called *Provo* – the grinning natural world in two-page spreads. Syl bent to look beneath the bed. His shoes. Some scientific journals. A coffee-cup. A tray of rocks. His binoculars. She ran her hand along the spines in his bookcase.

Finally she went downstairs into the kitchen, the most anonymous of rooms. Still nothing in the fridge to eat and drink. She'd have to go next door again, when it was morning, to beg some bread and cheese from her neighbour. For now the little drop of gleewater in its square bottle on the high shelf was worth the reaching after all. She was her father's height and shorter than Celice. She had to climb on to a chair. She blew the dust off the bottle's epaulettes, removed the stopper and drank the quarter measure without coming down off the chair. Too sugary. But energizing. There was a small round glass jar with a gold screw top hidden behind the spirit glasses at the back of the shelf, no bigger than a tangerine. Its contents looked like tiny yellow stones or shells. She took it down and held it to the ceiling light. Small rodent bones, perhaps. Misshapen pearls. Something from her mother's lab. Something they'd picked up on the beach, and kept, and hidden.

Syl unscrewed the cap and tipped the contents on her palm. They hardly weighed a gramme and felt as moist and soft as orange pips. They were all teeth, some as tiny and enamelled as a grain of rice, others larger, and contoured, spongy and pitted at their dentine caps but jagged and with the stringy residues of blood pulp on their roots. Milk teeth or 'fairy dice'. The sweet incisors, canines, molars of a girl.

She counted them, pushing them across her palm with one finger. Nineteen. One short of a set. That must be the one, Syl thought, that she had lost at school when she was about eleven. She had been worrying it all day with her tongue and thumb and it had almost fallen out while she was in the music class. Her teacher had insisted that she spit it in the lavatory and swill the blood away with water from the toilet tap. That one tooth had not been saved. But her mother and her father had preserved the rest, this first sign of their daughter's growing old.

Syl dropped her teeth back in the jar. Then, clutching it, she got down off the kitchen chair and went into the garden studio to curl up on the couch. Monday was approaching fast with its disjunctive ways. Monday rips the family apart. It sends its members off to work. It puts them on the bus and train and plane. She folded one hand round the jar of teeth and wrapped the other one around an ankle, spread her fingers on her lower leg, held herself in place with just her fingertips, dug bitten nails into her skin. She closed her eyes against the dawn to find out what it felt like to be loved and dead.

# 24

The brothers who ran the Salt Pines Company were happy to loan their sand jeep to the police. Although they hadn't yet started building a single house, their marketing campaign was due to open in ten days' time. Their brochures, already printed, had renamed the area Lullaby Coast, suggesting safety, retirement and the soothing presence of the sea. The murder of two respectable doctors of zoology on the fringes of the development could well suggest the opposite, that this was not a happy coast. It could suggest conspiracy as well. The doctors had publicly opposed the building scheme. Their names were on petitions. So the brothers would do what they could to remove the bodies from the dunes as speedily as possible and then persuade the police captain that a quiet, low-profile hunt for 'the responsibles' might well produce the best results for everyone.

Their driver took the vehicle along the coastal track then down the small stone jetty below the car park into the shallows of a receding tide where the sand was firmest and not too steeply banked. He would have liked to have accelerated and sent out loops of water from his tyres. Surf-driving. But this, he had been warned, would be the first, informal part of a funeral and he should drive the jeep as if it were a hearse. There were two empty coffins in the body of the jeep. So he kept the needle hovering at 10 k.p.h. and made the most of going through the waves as deeply as he dared, until he reached the first rocks of the bay and had to turn inland towards the dunes.

Two policemen showed him where to back and park. There were another two laying wooden duckboards along the sandy gully of the access dune, dull conscripts with unruly uniforms and minds. Three more men, in suits, and all with cigarettes, were standing like good golfing friends on the grass below the tent. The police detective. The magistrate. One of the brothers from Salt Pines. It looked as if they were expecting someone to come from the tent with a tray of drinks. Their conversation stopped when the thick green canvas had been loosened from its pegs and pulled off its shaking metal frame to show the sun-deprived rectangle of grass beneath. The tent had been up only since the Sunday morning. A day, that's all. But already photosynthesis had stalled. The lissom green had slightly paled, like the skin below a sticking plaster.

Celice and Joseph were still hidden under sheets and their refrigerating blankets, but nothing could disguise the smell. Bacon, seaweed, hoof-and-horn, the sweet-death odours of burnt marmalade. Six days of grace are more than anyone can bear. The three older men moved away and lit fresh cigarettes. One of the policemen – not allowed to smoke, but used to dirty work like this – handed round a tube of mints to his three colleagues and the driver. First they rolled the canvas up and jumped on it to pump out the envelopes of trapped air. Then they disconnected and took down the two fluorescent lamps from the top strut of the tent, and dismantled the twelve lengths of the frame. It took two men to drag the canvas down to the sand jeep. One other took the tent poles. The fourth carried the lighting battery. They returned along the duckboards with the two empty, wood-effect coffins on their shoulders. Provided by the city morgue, one standard issue for a man, a shorter one for a woman. The driver followed with the lids.

Filling the coffins would have been simple if the bodies had been laid on sheets, as well as covered by them. Then the policemen could easily make hammocks with which to lift and swing the victims into their boxes. But Joseph and Celice had not been moved, except by gulls and by the murderer, since they had died. The policemen would have to pull away their coverings and roll the bodies on to lengths of folded sheet. They put on plastic gloves. They did not want to touch the dead.

Celice, when she was finally exposed, was still chest down on the ground, her left cheek pressed into the lissom grass, her legs level with her husband's face, braced and supported on their toes and knees. Her upper body, in its black jacket and grubby white T-shirt made her seem the greater and the less-dead of the two. Below the waist she was as thin and leathery as a hermit's water-bag. The policemen did their best – but failed – to stop themselves from looking at her nakedness and at the chipped and flaking cherry red varnish of her nails.

Her husband's posture seemed the comic one. No clothes at all to keep him respectable. He was as modest as a beast. He'd fallen on his back. His legs were spread. His cock and testicles were livid mushrooms growing out of dough. His left wrist was twisted against the broken angle of his arm. And his hand was still wrapped round the stringy folds and sinews of her lower leg. Still devoted, then. Still in touch. But not quite innocent.

The murdered couple, in the weeks ahead, in the newspapers, even at the funeral, would have to shoulder some of the blame themselves. Their bodies were too compliant, unprotesting, over-dramatized. Their deaths – though ugly and gratuitous – seemed, even to the policemen gathered in the dunes, partly deserved. Wilful, even. Why had they wandered from the track? Why had they taken off their clothes, at such an age, in such a place, if not to draw the devils and the monsters to the dunes? These victims had been accomplices in their own misadventure. If life was an express that hurtled between termini, then it had been their choice to quit the moving train before the final station had been reached and dash themselves against the flying stillness of the earth. They'd courted death. And death had been seduced. They wanted it, and so it came, a hock of granite in its obliging hand. The four young policemen disapproved, as all the neighbours and the colleagues would. These people had been irresponsible, to let themselves be robbed so easily of their 'good deaths'. They should have laboured on until they'd reached the floating world of pain and age. They should have persevered and competed for the just rewards of death in bed.

The four young policemen, too close now to the pungent details of mortality to concentrate on anything but horrors of the flesh, were nauseous as they prepared to lift Celice and Joseph from the dunes. They coughed and gagged. They spat into the grass. They held their breath. Anything to keep the taste out of their mouths. This wasn't worth the pay. They'd rather be on traffic duty, even. Nevertheless they had no choice but to tuck the two sheets under the corpses, one to Joseph's left, the other to Celice's right. Twisting their heads to take deep lungfuls of air, two men to a body, they had to kneel down on the grass, spread their fingers against the rocky outcrops of the skull, the shoulder, the hip, the knee, and pull these two unlikely lovers apart. On to the sheets. Into their boxes, the one too large, the other far too short. Under their lids, and out of sight. Now the policemen could stand up and sip the sweet sea air.

What happened to our only prayer, *May no one come to lift his hand from her*? The power of a prayer is only brief at best. For a moment only, his arm was stretched as he clung on. His skin adhered. But soon his hand departed from her, slipping from the ankle bone. His fingers were unwoven through the heavy air. The space between them grew and grew. His knuckles dragged along the ground. Her lower leg was left with just the indent of his kissing fingertip. Joseph's body rolled towards the west. His wife went east. They came off the grass and on to cotton, then into wood-effect, then on to the flat bed of the sand jeep, along the beach and through the suburbs to the icy, sliding drawers of the city morgue, the coroner's far room, amongst the suicides. Their bodies had been swept away, at last, by wind, by time, by chance. The continents could start to drift again and there was space in heaven for the shooting stars.

If there were any justice in the world, there would be thunder, now that our only prayer has been betrayed, now that the light of time has been reunited with sound, its faster twin. Or else, at least, the baritone should sing. Lift up your voice, the conscience of the land. Protest. Give us your arias of grief. But there's no justice in the random and habitual parishes of death. The land is conscienceless. It has no ceremony. It cannot rise to the occasion, as people must, when there's a funeral. The best that it could do was wash its heavy waters on the shore, and stir the dunes where Joseph and Celice had died with its grey wind and let the daylight pop and crack with smaller lives than theirs.

What was their final legacy? A rectangle of faded grass and, where the bodies had decayed for their six days of grace, a crushed and formless smudge of almost white where time and night had robbed the lissom of its green.

# 25

**6.10 a.m.**

So this has been a *quivering* of sorts for Joseph and Celice. A day lived forwards has retrieved itself by fleeing from the future to the past. The dead are resurrected and they lie in bed at backward-running dawn, with first light of a perfect summer's day ducking and then dropping from the sky into the east, into the morning night. Ahead of them, the almost thirty years of married life, the more than twenty years before they met. The shrinking and retreating universe has left their deaths behind. They are not mortal any more.

Celice, in her wide bed, the shutters down, the silence broken by her whistling nose, is sleeping with the joyful certainty that Tuesday comes. Two days, alone, off work, with no alarm to wake her up and nothing she must do to fill her time except play music on the stereo, patrol the garden with her secateurs, walk down across the park, if it is fine, towards the shops, walk back to take some coffee and a cake at the Pavilion, toss crumbs amongst the birds, be free.

She is not restless in the least, or dreaming. Even her wheezing does not wake her up or nag her into turning on her side. She remembers in her subconscious exactly where her open book was dropped the night before and that her watch has slipped on to the floor. She will not roll on to the tasselled page-marker and crease it. She knows it's fallen there, by her shoulder, almost hidden by the pillow. If she wanted to she could even reach out in her sleep to find at once the crumpled tissue pushed into the tucking of the bed, to blow her nose or wipe her mouth or simply grip as a comforter.

The coverlet is pulled up to her chin. Her eyelids perch and shiver in the shadows of her face, pale resting moths. Her hair is spread across the pillow she once shared – and *quivering* will let her share again – with Syl and Joseph. If she is troubled or distressed by anything, if she is guilty or annoyed, or if her back and shoulders are painful, it does not show while she is asleep. She is too deep. She is too far away.

Joseph is the restless one, the fidgeter, in his more narrow bed in his untidy studio. He has a day of work ahead. Two meetings and a seminar. Two papers to prepare. A faculty report. Already he's aware of where he'll hurt that day. His knee is troublesome, even while he sleeps. His colon aches. He's having bladder dreams. He's almost praying for the day to come. Then he can piss the pain away and end the nightmare that has been haunting him since his last visit to the lavatory at twenty-five past four.

He is an old man in his dreams, racked with pain and naked in a pauper's bed. His hands are stiff. His fingertips have lost their sensitivity. All he can feel, when he has found the energy to push his hands beneath the sheets to try to reach and soothe the pain, is scaly skin. He has become pie-crust. It is a bore to be so old, and so condemned. But that – great age – is what he always wanted for himself. So here's his most sombre wish fulfilled.

His dream has moved him to the geriatric ward. The blankets

and the screens. They've plugged him in; a monitor, a catheter, a drip. He hears the trolleys in the corridor, the purring journeys of the hearse along embedded routes to one of death's ten thousand gates, and doctors saying, 'Let the old man die. The world turns mouldy otherwise.'

He calls her name, Celice. He does not want to die alone. He wants the blessing of warm light and the caressing touch of family. He wants the blinds pulled up, the candles lit, the shadows falling on his bed, the mutters of his people crowding at the door. He wants to hear the sobbing of his daughter and his wife and feel their fingers wrapped around his shin. Please, let them through, he whispers to himself. Then let me doze until you hear my half-completed breath and see the sweet narcosis of no dreams.

The house itself is stretching, creaky in the rousing wash of dawn's first grey. The sun's forehead is peeking at the day, its face still indigo from sleep, its cloudy head uncombed and tumbling its vapour curls on to the skyline of the sea. The birds are in the gardens now, throwing out long shadows from the peaks of trees. The town's first trams are nudging through the streets in search of love. The first alarms are sounding in a thousand homes. The water taps are opened and the gas fires lit. The smells are coffee, bread and soap. A crabbing boat is labouring along the coast, to meet the light half-way, or chase it back whence it came. And Joseph and Celice are in their rooms, spreadeagled in their beds. No matter how they toss and turn, no matter what they dream, no matter what the milky dark may whisper in their ears, its promises, its threats and its assurances, they can't avoid the coming and receding days of grace.

# 26

There was a tiger sky in the early hours of the morning – an orange wash of sun in mist behind a camouflage of black-grey, drifting stripes. The clouds were shredded by the wind. Later there would be rain, a middling tide and average temperatures. A dull and uninspiring day, except for a short storm in the afternoon when the sky would fill with lightning sprites and the sea would briefly turn to slate.

No one could tell that police had been at work, or what dramas had occurred the week before. Overnight, the weather and the sea had removed the spoors of the sand jeep, the duckboards and the policemen's boots. There was no evidence of humankind. The bay had been abandoned to itself, in its last months before Salt Pines.

It is, of course, a pity that the police dogs ever caught the scent of human carrion and led their poking masters to the dunes to clear away the corpses for 'proper burial', so that the dead could be less splendid in a grave. The dunes could have disposed of Joseph and Celice themselves. They didn't need help. The earth is practised in the craft of burial. It gathers round. It embraces and adopts the dead. Joseph and Celice would have turned to landscape, given time. Their bodies would have been just something extra dead in a landscape already sculpted out of death. They would become nothing special. Gulls die. And so do flies and crabs. So do the seals.

Even stars must decompose, disrupt and blister on the sky. Everything was born to go. The universe has learned to cope with death.

So, had it not been for the dogs, the residues of Joseph and Celice's lives would have been tossed and tumbled in the dunes to nourish and renew themselves in different forms. They might have found a brief eternity below the sand, together at first, still touching, but soon they'd have to separate, to weave and drift into the unremarking sea, or sink into the clods and pebbles of the earth. A slower journey than a hearse. Slower than a glacier.

Instead, they left only a white and yellow patch of lissom grass (or angel bed, pintongue, sand hair, repose) where they had loved and died, framed by a tent-made rectangle of lesser green. The bodies had blocked out the light and flattened and indented the soft ground underneath. For almost six days the grass had had to live by root alone, scavenging for nutrients and minerals with its thin threads while its foliage was bleaching in the dark. Celice and Joseph's long and heavy shapes had robbed the grass of its free energy and left a vegetable ghost. It was as if someone had thrown down a ship's tarpaulin or dragged up a skein of seaweed into the dunes for use as fertilizer on the fields and then collected it, days later, to leave their soft denials in the grass. Each blade was tendril soft, as colourless and feeble as a day-old shoot, as lank and listless as cut straw. Some leaves were bent and scarred and some were torn. Others had been pressed into the sandy earth, to seem ingrowing, keen to burrow back. The worms and grubs that hated light had come up to the surface for a change to crawl and slide in these rare caverns, leaving their half-tunnels and their casts as decorations on the ground. The smell was like red wine; earthy, rich and fermenting.

But once the tent and bodies were removed, and once the unsustaining night had passed, the wounded lissom grass perked up. Hope springs eternal in the natural world. Its leaves and blades sprang straight again. They dragged their bodies from the gluey sand to face the morning. They latched their protein-eyes on daylight. They photosynthesized. The grass's stored supplies of water and carbon dioxide conspired with the thin light of that misty, cloudy day to make its carbohydrates and put back into the world its by-product of oxygen. At last its bludgeoned chloroplasts could go about their work, capturing the energy of sunlight. They were the master craftsmen of the grass, the conjurors of chlorophyll. Gradually, as dawn was thickening, as day grew fat to slumber through the heavy afternoon, the pigments of the vegetable scar, its corpse stretched out across the grass, returned. By dusk the rectangle of time-paled lissom grass had gone. By dusk, next day, the ghost was sappy at its tips, and only yellow lower down where the leaves were closest to their stems. After that the lissom darkened, day after day. Spring green, then apple green. And bottle green. Envy green, and green as grass.

By final light on the ninth day since the murder all traces of any life and love that had been spilt had disappeared. The natural world had flooded back. The brightness of the universe returned. If there was any blood left in the soil from Joseph and Celice's short stay in the dunes then it could only help to fortify the living murmur of the grass.

\*

And still, today and every day, the dunes are lifted, stacked and undermined. Their crests migrate and reassemble with the wind. They do their best to raise their backs against the weather and the sea and block the wind-borne sorrows of the world. All along the shores of Baritone Bay and all the coast beyond, tide after tide, time after time, the corpses and the broken, thinned remains of fish and birds, of barnacles and rats, of molluscs, mammals, mussels, crabs are lifted, washed and sorted by the waves. And Joseph and Celice enjoy a loving and unconscious end, beyond experience.

These are the everending days of being dead.